WRONG TURN

PARADISE CRIME MYSTERIES PREQUEL NOVELLA 14

TOBY NEAL

Cover Design: Ebook Launch
Formatting: Jamie Davis

The wound is the place where the Light enters you.
— Rumi

CHAPTER ONE

Aunty Rosario narrowed her eyes at her niece and adopted daughter, twenty-one-year-old Lei Texeira. "You'll be careful? Mexico can be dangerous."

"Too careful, like I always am," Lei snorted, rolling a T-shirt neatly and tucking it into her duffle bag. "Glad I have Kelly to loosen me up."

Rosario fussed with a row of bird nests atop the bureau. Lei had been collecting them on their nature walks since her aunt had brought her, at age nine after her mother died, to the little bungalow on D Street in San Rafael, California. "I wish you girls had a boyfriend with you."

Lei turned to face her aunt, opening her mouth to challenge her guardian's sexist comment—but Rosario's cheeks were pale, and her brown eyes shadowed with worry. "Oh, Aunty." Lei dropped the shirt into the bag. "We'll be fine." She walked over to give the short, plump woman a hug, resting her cheek on her aunt's silver-streaked, curly hair. "Don't worry. I'll call you as soon as we reach the resort at Cabo San Lucas."

Rosario wrapped her arms around Lei's slender body, and squeezed. "It's the first time you've left me since you came."

Lei pulled back from her aunt. "Really?"

Rosario dropped her arms. "Really."

"Then it's past time I got on the road. I'm probably the only person my age who's never been anywhere without her guardian."

"Just—be careful."

"Don't forget—I've applied to the Hawaii police academy, Aunty. I'm going to be a cop. I can take care of myself, and Kelly too." Lei resumed packing, reaching for her sensible one-piece swimsuit. "I'm more worried about leaving *you* here. This neighborhood has been going downhill." A series of break-ins nearby had put them on high alert. "Those robbers don't seem to care that people are home when they break in."

"I can't imagine anyone would break into this house." Rosario flapped a hand dismissively. "I know everyone on my street, and everyone knows me because of the restaurant. Momi and Deke will be checking in on me, too." Aunty Rosario ran a popular Hawaiian food restaurant nearby. Rosario's business partner, Momi, and her husband were like extended family. Rosario looked at Lei. "But I do have an idea I think you'll like, for when you get back."

"Oh yeah?" Lei shoved a pair of jeans into the duffle and zipped it up. "If it's something to keep me from moving to the Big Island, Aunty, I'm sorry but I've made up my mind. I need to return to—where it all began."

"I know, Lei-girl." Rosario straightened the bird nests one more time, and sighed. "I understand why. With your father in jail and your mother dead of the drugs—I know why you need to go back to Hawaii and be a part of making things better there. It's good for you to go on a little vacation, have fun like girls your age do; I worry, that's all." She looked up and caught Lei's eye. "But I thought of something that could help us when you get back."

A car horn tooted from outside the house. "That's Kelly!" Lei exclaimed. "I have to go, Aunty." She grabbed the duffle and headed for the door.

Rosario stopped Lei, resting her hands on the young woman's shoulders. "Don't you want to hear my idea?"

"Of course, Aunty." Lei made herself hold still, stifling her impatience. "Tell me."

"I think we should get a dog. A police dog. People can adopt animals that didn't make it through the K-9 training program."

Lei frowned. "I don't know. Sounds like a lot of responsibility. Let's talk about it in ten days." She kissed her aunt's forehead. "Love you, Aunty! I'll be back before you know it."

Lei hurried out of the bedroom, down the hall and out the front door, waving to her pretty blonde friend waiting in the red Mustang convertible parked in front of the house. "All right, Kelly. Let's get this party started!"

CHAPTER TWO

THREE DAYS LATER, Lei pressed down on the accelerator, and the bright red convertible surged forward. Hot wind tossed her curly hair. Desert streamed by, populated by saguaro cactuses and tumbleweeds. Beside her, Kelly shrieked with glee at the speed, leaping up in her seat to throw her arms in the air. "Yeehaw!"

Lei flicked a glance at her friend, smiling. "You gotta lose that Texas speak."

"Heck no! And y'all better know it!" Kelly sat back down. "How far to the resort?"

"Another hour or so."

"This has been the perfect road trip."

The girls had left the Bay Area three days before, tooling down Highway One along the Big Sur coast, spending a night in Pismo Beach and another in Los Angeles. They'd crossed the border into Mexico some hours ago.

"And we're just getting to the real fun—the margaritas and cabana boys." Lei throttled back, pulling in behind a jacked-up pickup filled with rooster cages. A couple of pit bulls lolled their tongues out the back, panting in the heat. Lei smiled at the sight.

This Mexican scene could be straight out of her old neighborhood on the Big Island of Hawaii, where she'd grown up.

Kelly pulled slim tanned legs up onto the seat, propping open the glossy Cabo San Lucas brochure on her knees. "Five days and four nights of epic partying. I'm ready for the dancing and dating."

"Me too," Lei said, suppressing a quiver of doubt. Kelly had begged for them to go for a real vacation during spring break, after a heavy semester at their college. Lei was working on a Bachelor's in Criminal Justice and Kelly was completing a nursing degree. An unlikely pairing, the girls had hit it off in one of their first general ed classes. Kelly, from a wealthy Texas clan that had moved to California in her senior year of high school, had latched onto prickly, loner Lei—and somehow the friendship worked.

"I wish you didn't have such an eyesore of a car, though," Lei complained. "We could take out a billboard advertising what tourists we are. Seriously, we could always tell in Hawaii, whenever we saw one of these, that someone was 'off the boat.'"

Lei was proud to be a local Hawaii girl: half Japanese, one-quarter Hawaiian, and one-quarter Portuguese. The mix of races had given her unique looks: curly brown hair, big, tilted eyes, freckled olive skin, and a lean runner's build.

"Hey. I'm not ashamed of who I am," Kelly said. "Got big hair and big boobs, too." She bounced, illustrating her words. "I've never understood your need to blend in."

"*No act,*" Lei said. "A saying we have in Hawaii. Means don't get above yourself. Standing out isn't a good thing. It can be dangerous, too, in a place like this." Lei gestured to the barren landscape. Lei already knew too much about the many ways people could prey on each other. "Fortunately, we're on a pretty major road."

"But how are we going to get any action except by getting attention?" Kelly set the resort brochure back in the side pocket of the car's door. "I'm looking for some fun. That's why we've got separate rooms—I plan on some chandelier swinging and wall banging, and not by myself, either."

Lei chuckled. "Thank God we have separate rooms, then." She smiled at her friend, but that quiver tightened her belly again. She, too, hoped to meet someone nice and have fun—but she was way too messed up to just bring someone back to the room for sex. On the other hand, she didn't want to be tied up in knots about it anymore, either. She was determined to get past the hang-ups that Charlie Kwon, her mother's drug-dealing boyfriend, had given her through his abuse. "You fall down, girl, you get back up," Aunty Rosario always said.

They reached a crossroads. Lei slowed to a stop under a blinking red light that dangled between a couple of poles. "Can you check the GPS? I think we keep going straight here, but we should see the ocean by now."

"Sure." Kelly set down the bottle of tanning lotion she'd been applying to her shoulders and picked up her phone. "Shoot. We lost signal when we crossed the border, but I brought a map. Pull over so I can look at it."

Lei eased the Mustang onto the soft, sandy shoulder as Kelly unfolded the map. She stayed alert, watching the other cars and trucks approach and move on. Most of the traffic treated the red light as a mere suggestion. A pickup full of young men wolf-whistled and called out compliments in Spanish, along with crude hand gestures.

"Hurry up, Kelly!" Lei slid down out of sight in her seat, getting more nervous by the minute at their vulnerable position.

"It's another thirty miles, and we need to make a right here." Kelly folded the map at last. "Good thing we stopped."

Lei pressed the gas pedal and hit the signal for a left turn back onto the asphalt—but when she accelerated, the rear-wheel drive of the sports car lost traction in the sand. She increased the gas, but the tires just spun, spraying sand behind the vehicle. Lei turned the wheel back and forth, seeking purchase with the front tires, but instead they seemed to be working themselves deeper.

"Shinola!" Kelly exclaimed, not one for swearing. A large,

battered Ford truck pulled up in front of them with a winch on the rear bumper. "Hey. Maybe they're stopping to help us."

CHAPTER THREE

Two Hispanic men with lots of tattoos got out of the Ford. Lei stopped the useless spinning of the tires and sat, hands clenched on the wheel, teeth gritted, as Kelly smiled and waved. They ignored scowling Lei and smiled at Kelly.

"*Hola!*" Kelly chirped. "*Habla inglés?*"

"*Un poco.*" The first man reached them. "We help you." Long hair touched his shoulders, and a silver chain the width of a finger dangled across a chest he was clearly proud of as he flexed for them in a thin white undershirt. He leaned an arm on the frame of the windshield and gazed down at Kelly admiringly. "What's your name, *chica?*"

The other man approached Lei's side. Short, with a shaved, shiny head, thick neck, and the broad shoulders of a wrestler, he reminded Lei of a Hispanic Vin Diesel. Probably someone's nice dad or uncle, here to give aid, she hoped—but the expression in the man's dark eyes was speculative rather than friendly as they ran over her, the car, and Kelly.

Lei glanced around for anyone else noticing what was going on. Traffic continued to whiz by without slowing.

"We pull you out, *no problemo*," Silver Chain told Kelly. "Me Joao. This Fernando." He gestured to the bald man.

"*Gracias*, Joao! *Me llamo* Kelly. And this is Lei." Kelly's limited Spanish failed as she gestured.

"*Hola.*" Lei inclined her head stiffly, inhaling a strong waft of unwashed armpit from Joao's direction.

The bald man named Fernando returned to the truck and fiddled with the winch on the back, unspooling a length of cable connected to a heavy steel hook. Lei craned her neck to see what he was doing as he flattened out in the sand and reached under the front bumper with the hook. She heard a clunking sound as he got the hook secured.

Fernando stood up and dusted sand off his hands. His eyes gleamed, and he smiled for the first time. She felt his gaze on her like a touch, and the back of her neck prickled with alarm.

"No," Lei said loudly. "Unhook that winch right now. We don't want your help. No *ayuda!*" Lei had brought the Glock she'd bought and was learning to use for when she began her job as a police officer. She had a knife too, but both were sensibly locked in a case in the glove box.

"We do want help," Kelly argued. "It'll take them two seconds to pull us out, Lei!"

Joao continued to grin, and Fernando winked at Lei without responding to her words. He got back into the truck and turned it on with a roar.

"Put it in neutral," he yelled out the window to Lei. She did, surprised at his easy English.

"I ride with you *chicas*." Joao jumped with unnerving speed into the back seat, not bothering with the door. "Where we go?"

"*We're* going to Cabo." Kelly scrunched her brows. "But no need for you to ride with us. Go back to your truck, please."

Lei wanted to get her weapon; but to do that she had to turn off the car and use the key to unlock the glove box, not to mention getting the Glock out of its case, all of which would alert Joao to her intentions.

Joao just grinned and settled himself. He spread thick, ripped arms out along the convertible's rear seat, tipping back his head in exaggerated enjoyment.

Kelly glanced at Lei with worry in her wide blue eyes.

The truck, clearly already in four-wheel drive, bit into the sand and lurched forward. The cable tightened, jerking the Mustang and throwing the girls into each other. Joao leaned forward between the seats. Beery breath fanned Lei's cheek. "Fun, no?"

The truck accelerated against the pull of the trapped car, belching gas fumes as it got its tires onto the pavement. A moment later, it hauled the Mustang easily out of the sand. Fernando eased the truck forward slowly as Lei steered the convertible onto the road.

"*Gracias*," Kelly said to Joao with a big, fake smile. "Now you go back to your truck. Thank you." She dug in her pretty red clutch purse. "I'll get you something for your trouble."

Fernando wasn't stopping now that he'd got them up onto the pavement.

Instead, the truck sped up. The Mustang surged forward, and Lei tightened her hands on the steering wheel. "Oh, shit."

Joao leaned forward between the seats, ogling Kelly's abundant cleavage. "You *chicas* like party? We go party."

"No. We have somewhere to be, and people expecting us," Lei said. *They had to get away from these guys.*

Lei engaged the Mustang's engine, putting the vehicle in gear, and braked.

The cable connecting the vehicles hummed. The Mustang fishtailed, its bumper knocking back and forth against the truck's much sturdier rear end. Kelly screamed, grabbing the dash.

Joao, tossed around in back, reached forward and grabbed Lei's hair, pulling her head back as a large Buck knife appeared in his hand. She felt the chill of the blade against her neck.

"Car in neutral," he growled. "Foot off the brake." The tip of the knife broke Lei's skin, and the heat of blood warmed her clammy neck.

"Oh my god!" Kelly screamed. "Stop it, you're hurting her!"

Lei needed to buy time to get to her weapons; she couldn't take a chance on getting her throat slit right now. She slid the gearshift down, moving the Mustang back into neutral, and took her foot off the brake. The convertible straightened out obediently. The desert flashed by in a blur.

"Give me your phones."

"No!" Kelly exclaimed. Joao nicked Lei's ear with the knife. Lei shut her eyes at the sting; more blood spattered her bare shoulder. "Okay, okay!"

"Your friend's, too."

Kelly handed Joao her phone, then took Lei's off the console. Joao tossed both phones over his shoulder; they were moving too fast to hear their lifeline to help crunching into oblivion on the highway behind the speeding car.

CHAPTER FOUR

"No hands on the wheel," Joao said. Lei let go. "Blondie. Tie her hands." Kelly grimaced as he poked Lei's neck again, threatening. "Tie her hands, bitch."

"No, I won't. I don't have anything . . ."

Joao gestured impatiently to the leather belt studded with silver conchas threaded through Kelly's denim shorts. Kelly pulled the belt off and wound it around Lei's hands, buckling the leather tight in a crude restraint. "I'm sorry," Kelly said. "You were right. We should have got out and ran."

"Shut up!" Joao snarled.

The truck towing them continued to pick up speed. The Mustang wove slightly in its wake, hurtling toward wherever these men were taking them.

Lei felt herself lift out of her body into that place she went when things got bad as Joao held her head back and played with her hair, his fingers tangled in the riot of her windblown curls, his hot breath on her neck. Her stomach clenched as he licked her wounded ear and tickled her with the knife, clearly enjoying her vulnerability—but Lei was buffered from it.

This nightmare was happening to *Damaged Goods*—DG, Kwon

had always called her. He'd called her that even in front of her mother, who thought it stood for Dear Girl.

Kelly moaned in terror. Lei wished she could tell her friend not to let on, that such sounds only encouraged men like this—but it was too late.

"Come. *Aqui.* You sit with me, Blondie," Joao told Kelly, patting his lap.

Kelly curled herself away in response, and he reached down beside her seat and pushed the lever. The seat reclined abruptly, and Kelly fell backward with a squeal. Joao let go of Lei and grabbed Kelly by the long tresses she was so proud of, pulling her backward into the seat with him. "Nice Blondie," he said. "We party."

Lei blocked out the sounds of her friend being molested by scanning around for some way to get help. A glance at the speedometer showed that they were going sixty miles an hour, so jumping was out of the question. Even if she regained control of the Mustang, trying to get loose at this speed would likely flip or tear the car apart.

But maybe Lei could get the attention of another driver? Lei spent a couple of interminable minutes trying to signal cars passing them too rapidly to register the struggle happening in the convertible.

Joao now had Kelly down out of sight in the back seat, her friend's muffled cries raking Lei's nerves. Lei peeked around the seat and got a glimpse of Joao's hand on one of Kelly's bare breasts, his other around her throat.

At least he'd put down the knife, too occupied with rape to bother with it. He thought he'd neutralized Lei—but she could stop this. She had to find a way.

Lei fumbled for the opening of the glove box, hoping by some miracle it wasn't locked—but she'd closed the weapons in there with the car key, worried Kelly would find them and question her about bringing them. She'd sweated through lying about carrying a gun at the border crossing—Lei was not a good liar—but now she'd have to turn the Mustang off, remove the key, unlock the box, take out the case, and get the weapon out—all with bound hands and Joao not noticing.

Kelly gave a muffled scream, and the car bounced and fishtailed with the scuffle going on in the back seat.

There had to be something more immediate Lei could do.

She spotted the steel thermos in the wheel well that they'd filled with margarita mix this morning. Awkward with her tied hands, Lei picked it up. She swiveled, pushing herself upright, leaning between the seats, and lifted the thermos high.

Joao held Kelly down with a bent forearm against her throat, suffocating her as he fumbled with his pants zipper with the other hand. He was no longer paying attention to anything but what was between his legs.

Lei's eyes met Kelly's terrified ones as she brought the thermos down on Joao's head with all her strength.

Joao collapsed over Kelly without a whisper.

Her friend gasped for air as Joao's arm went slack. Kelly shoved at his body, whimpering and frantic. "Get him off me. Get him off me!" Kelly croaked. Tears streamed down her face.

Lei dropped the thermos and wriggled between the seats, picking up the huge combat knife that Joao had set aside.

"Untie my hands," Lei said. Kelly plucked at the buckled belt around Lei's wrists, freeing her, as Lei kept a wary eye on the unconscious Joao.

The convertible slowed. Lei swiveled around to look at the truck towing them. "Oh no. He must see something's wrong."

But that wasn't it.

Fernando was merely turning off the main highway onto a dirt road. Pale dust belched up around them as the Mustang bucked through potholes at a much slower speed. Lei helped haul Joao's body off Kelly, wedging him facedown onto the car's floor area.

"Kill him!" Kelly exclaimed. Lei looked down at the man before her. *It would be easy to cut his throat, stab him.* A part of her longed to, but she shook her head.

TOBY NEAL

"No. We still have to get out of this mess. We're toast if we kill him now, in a foreign country, with Fernando to deal with. We need to neutralize him, though." Lei pulled Joao's arms up behind his back and wrapped the belt ruthlessly tight around his wrists. "He made a mistake leaving my hands in front. He underestimated us."

"He underestimated *you*." Kelly's teeth were chattering. "I was just the idiot you've always said I am."

"You expect the best of people," Lei said. "I know better, that's all. Now that we're going slower, let's see if we can get loose from the truck. You push Joao out into the road."

"I can't lift him," Kelly panted. "How can I get him out?"

"Then stay down, out of sight. I need to make sure Fernando doesn't realize what's going on. He has to think you guys are getting it on back there."

"You mean, I'm getting raped," Kelly said. "This is so disgusting." She grunted with the effort of trying to move Joao. "I can't get him up off the floor. It's going to take both of us."

Lei turned to see what Fernando was up to, glancing at the clock on the dash. The whole struggle had taken less than five minutes.

The bald man had a mirror trained on them, and she noticed the gleam of light on his jaw, the glowing ember of a cigarette in his mouth. He glanced back, and she met his eyes with a glare. He took the cigarette out of his mouth and made a kissing gesture.

Lei shuddered.

Where had Fernando secured the hook under the car? Clearly, it was somewhere a lot sturdier than the Mustang's plastic bumper, which was more for looks than function.

She needed her weapon. With the gun, Lei could force Fernando to let them go.

Lei made sure the Mustang was still in neutral and turned off the engine. She took the key from the ignition and inserted it into the glove box.

"Help me," Kelly grunted from behind her. "I've almost got him up against the door."

"Let me get my weapon first." Lei turned the key.

"What?" Kelly exclaimed.

"My gun. It's locked in the glove box." The key refused to turn. Lei jiggled it impatiently.

Suddenly the Mustang slewed, swinging sideways and crashing into the truck's rear bumper as Fernando put on the brakes. Kelly cried out as she was flung against a door, and Lei sprawled across the front seats. The keys fell from her hand and slid under the passenger side seat as the Mustang swung and hit the back of the truck from the other direction.

Lei smacked her head on the dash and the gearshift dug into her ribs, but she scrambled for the key anyway, popping her seatbelt and heaving herself headfirst downward, to search under the seat.

The car came to a jarring halt.

Lei got ahold of the keys and reached up, shoving the glove box key in. She turned it.

The driver's side door yanked open. Lei heaved herself over to look up. Fernando stared down at her in consternation, then reached for her.

CHAPTER FIVE

LEI KICKED OUT AT FERNANDO, connecting with his belly, which felt like granite under her athletic shoe. The bald man's expression went dark as his eyes narrowed and mouth tightened. He grabbed both her ankles, and despite Lei's thrashing, hauled her out of the vehicle with one powerful heave of muscle-bound arms.

Lei landed on her face in the dirt road, the breath knocked out of her. Spangles of light spun in her vision as she tried to get a breath, her hand scrabbling down to reach for Joao's knife in her pocket.

"Leave her alone!" Kelly shrieked, and jumped out of the car onto Fernando. She clung to the man's back, swatting at his shiny pate and trying to grab his ears. Fernando ignored her, much as a rhino does a fly, assessing the situation with his tree trunk legs spread and arms akimbo. "Joao!" he barked.

The other man groaned from the back seat. *"Putas!"*

Fernando grunted. *"Si.* But they have their uses." Kelly had begun to slide down the wall of his back. Fernando reached around and plucked her off, smacking her hard on the side of the head. Lei finally got a breath and scrambled to her feet, just in time to see her friend knocked out from the blow. Fernando tucked Kelly under his arm like a limp kitten, walked over and threw her into the cab of the truck; Kelly's head thumped against the doorframe.

Lei ran to the opposite side of the Mustang from Fernando. With the car between them, she felt able to engage him a little bit.

"Let us go. We have connections in the United States. We can pay, but you're going to get in big trouble if you hurt us." She pulled Joao's Buck knife out of her pocket and waved it threateningly. Truth was, she had no idea how to use it—she'd been planning to take lessons at some point in the future, if she ever lived to be a cop.

Fernando gave her a dismissive glance. He opened the back door of the Mustang. "Get out, you idiot," he told Joao; Lei was able to understand with her high school Spanish.

The other man complied, wriggling gracelessly out of the vehicle and heaving himself to his feet. Fernando snorted at the sight of his bound arms and loosened fly. "Thinking with your dick again. You were supposed to wait."

Joao shrugged. "I didn't want to wait."

Fernando pulled a knife at least as big as Lei's out of a scabbard at his waist. He slashed through the concha belt binding Joao's arms like it was spaghetti, and the leather fell to the ground. Joao shook out his bulky shoulders, flexing his hands.

Both men turned to face her.

Joao's eyes slitted with rage as Lei waved his knife at him. "You're mine, bitch," he snarled, stalking around one side of the car toward her.

Fernando smiled. His expression scared her more than Joao's as the bald man circled the vehicle from the other side. "No. You can have the blonde. This one's mine. I like 'em with a little fight."

"Oh, shit," Lei muttered, glancing back and forth between them. "Oh shit."

She spun on a heel and made a break for it, straight into the desert.

The area around the dirt road was sandy soil, dotted with the round balls of tumbleweeds and desert sage with an occasional barrel cactus or saguaro adding an extra hazard as Lei ran.

She had one advantage over the men—*she ran a lot.*

Terror gave her extra speed and she tore through the sagebrush and sand, leaping over a small barrel cactus in her path like a hurdler, never looking back to see if they were catching up to her. Lei's only advantage was speed, and she couldn't waste it.

Lei could hear them behind her: panting breath, crunching brush, the occasional curse. She focused on the ground directly ahead of her, thankful that she'd worn her usual outfit of athletic shorts, tank shirt, and a pair of running shoes, in spite of Kelly's teasing to get into a cuter outfit.

The sounds of pursuit grew fainter. She was leaving them behind, and it was a good thing too, because she was reaching the limits of her endurance. She hurtled up the long swell of a brush-covered sand dune, breath tearing through overworked lungs.

She reached the top and turned, slowing her steps. Her shoes sank in loose, deep sand as she paused, leaning over to rest her hands on her knees and look back.

The two men were already returning to the car, and a moment later, Fernando looked right at Lei in her place on the dune as he opened the door of the truck. He reached in and pulled Kelly up by her hair. Looking right at Lei, he flourished his huge Buck knife against her friend's neck. Lei gasped, covering her mouth with her hands.

He was trying to make her return, by holding Kelly hostage.

But if Lei went back, he'd just have two girls to torture—and if Lei found help, one of them at least might survive.

Was she justifying leaving Kelly there to suffer alone? Lei's mouth was chalky with the horror of her dilemma.

She took too long to decide.

Slower on his feet, Joao finally reached the vehicle. She saw the men exchange angry words, and Joao got in. Fernando waved the knife toward Lei again, and then unceremoniously shoved Kelly into the middle of the seat between the men and climbed in, too, slamming the door. The truck fired up and drove away, churning dust over the red Mustang still fishtailing in its wake.

"Oh no." Leis knees buckled, and she sat abruptly. "Poor Kelly. I have to help her."

But how? She was in the middle of nowhere, in the desert, without water or a cell phone. She hung her head for a moment, getting her breath and her bearings, shaking with delayed shock. She stood up and hiked the few more feet to the top of the dune.

From that vantage point, Lei could see back to the road, an empty line through the desert that led toward the mountains. Those hills were arid and shadowed with shades of mauve, blue and dusty green as afternoon waned. In the other direction, the ocean gleamed in the distance, cool and taunting, behind a bank of dunes.

Might as well head that way. Where there was a beach, there was the possibility of people, and she was afraid to return to that rough, empty road.

Lei slid and sank down the loose sand on the front of the dune and labored over two more before she saw an unexpected sight: another sandy road, and a large, battered sign advertising *TACOS DELICIOSO*.

"Tacos," Lei murmured. "And water." The thought of biting into a tasty taco washed down with cool water got her moving again. Where there were tacos, there were people.

Lei was hot, sticky, and thirsty past the point of discomfort when she stumbled into an empty parking area in front of a low cement block home. A couple of lonely picnic tables painted the same blue as the sign marked this isolated spot as the taco place. The ocean glittered off in the distance beyond yet another dune. A rusty RV, the kind built on the back of a truck, was parked to one side, tires half-buried in drifting sand.

No one appeared to be around.

Lei's mouth was too dry even to call out for help as she collapsed at one of the picnic tables. She lowered her head to her crossed arms. She'd just rest a minute before she looked for a way to communicate.

A deep growl raised the hairs on the back of her neck.

Lei turned very slowly. She faced a large German shepherd dog. A handsome buff and black, his intelligent brown eyes gazed at Lei unblinking, as a black lip drew up to reveal gleaming white teeth. Lei could feel the rumble of the dog's growl through the wood of the table.

"Good boy." Lei pitched her voice low, which wasn't hard given her dehydrated state. "You're just surprised I'm here. Come get scratches." She extended her hand slowly in a fist, fingers down.

The shepherd approached, the growl dimming, his ruff settling. He sniffed her hand, then sat and bumped his head under her fist. Obediently, she scratched behind his ears.

"You look all bad, but you're just a big sweetheart." This dog was just her type: large and protective, but with a sweet side.

"He doesn't usually like strangers." A young woman stepped down from the back of the RV; she was long-legged and brown, with a tumble of black hair past her shoulders. Lei paused, and the dog butted her hand until she scratched him again. His coat looked rough, but felt soft as lamb's wool under her hand.

"I approached on foot. I'm sure that's unusual." She was being assessed, and she gazed right back as the woman approached, moving with the springy grace of an athlete. "Is he your dog?"

"Yes. His name is Kona." The woman wore an outfit similar to Lei's—athletic shorts and a tank top. No shoes. Deeply tanned skin hinted at an ethnic heritage and made the woman's light brown eyes stand out dramatically, framed by that wild black hair falling over shoulders tight with muscle. "My name's Harry. Harriet Vierra."

"My name's Lei—and I need help." Lei's voice cracked with strain, and her hand tightened in the dog's fur. "I ran here through the desert. My friend and I were attacked by some asshole rapists. They stole the car and they have my friend. Do you have a phone to call the police?"

A long moment passed as Harry stared at Lei, then she made a gesture with her head. "Come into my RV. I'll give you something to drink, and you can tell me what happened." Lei got up and followed her inside the battered vehicle. Just to be out of the sun was a relief as Lei stepped up into the trailer—she could feel the freckles that had come out on her nose burning, even in the shade.

The space inside was cramped, but perfectly tidy and in much better shape than the exterior. The woman opened a tiny refrigerator and took out a jug of what looked like lemonade, splashing a plastic cup full of the cool liquid. The drink tasted like heaven going down. Lei felt the warm burn of alcohol on her throat—she was drinking a homemade margarita, and it was ambrosia. She tipped the cup and finished it to the last drop.

Harry sipped her drink, eying Lei over the edge of the cup. "Lei —that name sounds Hawaiian."

"I'm one-fourth." Lei held out her cup for a refill. "Half Japanese, and another fourth Portuguese."

"Classic local girl blend. Interesting to meet you out here—I'm half Hawaiian." Harry refilled Lei's cup.

That too was unusual, but they didn't have time to swap stories. Lei was here to get help for Kelly. She mustered her scattered attention. "My friend Kelly and I were on a road trip, coming down here to Cabo for spring break." Lei, loosened up by relief and tequila, quickly told the sorry tale.

"What direction did the men go down the road?" Harry turned and opened a cabinet. Reaching in, she took out a pistol. It was an old-fashioned six-shot Colt, and Lei frowned as the woman flipped open the barrel, pulled a box of ammo out of the cabinet, and slid bullets into the circular chamber.

"They went inland, farther toward the mountains. Do you have a phone? We have to call the police," Lei said.

"No phone out here. The folks in the house don't have one either." The woman pointed with her chin toward the bunkerlike house. She snapped the Colt's chamber shut.

Lei's pulse accelerated—what was Harry doing with that gun? They had to get moving! "I need to get help, somehow! Kelly's been kidnapped, and it would be a miracle if she hasn't already been raped by now. One of the men, Fernando, tried to get me to come back to the car by holding her up by the hair. He did this." She made the throat-cutting gesture the thug had used, her skin crawling with fear for Kelly. "I was lucky to be able to take this off one of them." Lei pulled out Joao's large knife in its scabbard and set it on the table. Harry picked it up, turning it back and forth. Lei well remembered the bite of the shiny steel on the skin of her neck.

"Not likely they're going to kill her. Maybe ransom her or sell her off to a brothel. Fernando and Joao, eh? What did they drive?"

"A big Ford truck with a winch." Lei held out her cup for more of the margarita. Harry obligingly filled her cup again.

"Well, I know that road you were on, and where it goes. I'm sorry about your friend." There was a note of finality in Harry's voice, as if whatever were being done to Kelly was already an irreversible fact. "But we can get her back."

Lei frowned. "Seriously? What can we do against those guys?"

"The cops are useless here. In fact, your perps could be off-duty cops trolling for victims. We call for help, you'll likely end up in jail and never hear from your friend again, unless you've got a wad of cash for bribes." Harry raked Lei with a glance. "Got a wad of cash?"

"No." Lei turned out her empty pockets. "I don't even have an ID right now."

"We're better off without the cops. Trust me." Harry stood up from the vinyl-covered bench seat of the dinette area, a tiny nook off the back of the truck.

"Are you telling me you're thinking of going after those guys with that little six-shooter of yours? You don't know what we're up against. I'm pretty strong, been taking *taekwondo* for a couple of years and I'm planning to be a cop, but this bald guy Fernando threw me around like a rag doll. Only reason I got away is that they didn't have guns, and I'm a fast runner."

Harry's brown eyes lit with excitement. "I guess you think we need a few more weapons." She gestured for Lei to get up off the seat.

Lei did. Harry lifted up the seat pad. Lei sucked in a breath of admiration. A shotgun, a rack of various pistols, with and without silencers, a knife the size of a machete, a brace of grenades, and a small rocket launcher packed the container area. Harry gestured. "Pick your poison."

Lei looked up. "Who *are* you?"

The Hawaiian woman shrugged. "Harry Vierra. That's all you need to know."

CHAPTER SIX

LEI TURNED her face to the side, pressing it against Harry's shoulder to block out the dusty wind churned up by the all-terrain vehicle they rode. Lei's back felt heavy with the backpack of weapons she carried. She shut her eyes against the grit as the ATV tackled yet another dune.

"I think I know where they're going," Harry had told her back at the RV as she began loading and packing the weapons they chose and they waited for the light to wane into darkness. "There's an old copper mine at the base of the mountains, where that road you were on dead-ends. No one lives there anymore, but it would be an ideal place to stash a prisoner."

"Yeah. No one to hear her scream," Lei said morosely. "Can't we get going now?"

Harry just looked at her, and Lei sighed. "I know. Waiting for dark. As if the deck wasn't already stacked against us."

"It isn't stacked against us." Harry shrugged into an odd harness. Lei frowned curiously until Harry picked up a short samurai-type sword in a slightly curved scabbard that had been stashed behind the seat cushion. Harry slid the scabbard into the harness. The hilt protruded up behind her head for easy access. "My trainer, Cruz, left his blade. He's away for the weekend, so I think I'll take it."

Lei shook her head. "I like these." She patted twin Glocks she'd chosen, wearing them in a pair of crossed shoulder holsters. Lei had been shooting at her local range with the Glock she'd bought but didn't know how to use half of Harry's arsenal. "You're still just getting trained? In what, exactly?"

"Combat techniques. Weapons. Tracking. Surveillance and sabotage. We've even done some explosives work. I graduated. I think. With Cruz, it's hard to tell."

"Why would you be out here studying all that?"

Harry quirked a brow. "Reasons. You're not the only one interested in a career in criminal justice."

"So who is this Cruz?"

"A ninja. A warrior. Maybe a monk of some kind. I don't know. He's a man of mystery. And he's got mad skills."

Lei fiddled with the holsters. "So Cruz came with you to Mexico? Like—a boyfriend?"

"Ha. Cruz is nobody's boyfriend. No, we met down here and I hired him to train me. We began doing private security jobs together." Harry shot up, strode to the refrigerator, grabbed the beaker of margaritas. "More?"

"Just water now. I should keep a clear head." Lei frowned. "You never answered me when I asked—who are you? Why are you doing this?"

"I'm a private investigator and a security operative—a bit of both." Harry shrugged. "Our most recent job was kind of like getting your friend back, actually. Cruz and I removed a kidnapped kid from a cartel that was holding her. Kona and I were on post-operation R & R when you showed up, but I guess it's time to go back to work."

Lei's nape prickled. She refilled her cup with water, her eyes narrowing. "This is too coincidental. What are the chances that the first place I come to, I happen upon a trained merc? You might be part of the gang—maybe you're going to lure me into going back with you to those guys."

Harry tipped her head and laughed; she had a robust belly laugh, and she was beautiful with her face alight. "You've already had too much to drink, I see. Let's go next door and get some food; the Delgados can vouch for me, and that will make you feel better."

Back in the present moment, Lei tightened her hold on Harry's narrow waist as the quad hit a protruding rock. They levitated, bouncing back down in a flurry of sand. Lei glanced behind her. Kona was hunkered down in a makeshift metal carrier strapped onto the back of the quad. The big dog's ears were flat, his eyes slitted. He lay low, his claws dug into the basket, tension in every line of his rough-coated body.

Lei peered around Harry to the terrain ahead. The last waning of sunset left orange streaks in the sky behind them. The moon rose ahead, glowing over the mountains above the abandoned mine.

Harry had changed into a desert camouflage outfit. She smelled like gun oil and sweat. She couldn't be more different than Kelly. Lei shut her eyes tight at the thought of her fun-loving, naive, sheltered friend, and what those men were likely doing to her. Every minute she'd taken with the Delgados, the friendly couple that ran the taco stand, eating a big plate of enchiladas, was time she'd wasted coming to Kelly's aid—but it had seemed important to verify that Harry had been coming to Mexico to spend the winter for several years, but only recently had taken up crime-fighting. "She was a bookkeeper before," Senor Delgado said. "We love her like a daughter." He gave Harry a side hug that almost buried her in his bulk. They hadn't had a phone, either—Harry had told the truth about that.

"A bookkeeper?" Lei had said, with raised eyebrows, as they went to fetch the ATV.

"For the mob," Harry said.

Lei didn't ask any more questions—a world of possibility lay in those three short words.

Harry aimed the ATV down a dune and finally merged onto the

road leading into a mining ghost town. The quad sped up, and Lei tucked her face tight into Harry's shoulder, watching the moonlit desert speed by now that they were on a relatively hard surface. The outline of the sword was an uncomfortable ridge between them.

Harry was so far out that she made Lei feel normal. Lei smiled a little at the thought. She usually felt so different from other women—not just because of being damaged goods, but because something in her wanted to right the balance of things, and she never was able to let that go.

That part of her was excited by this wild ride on an ATV through the back roads of Mexico, armed to the teeth; but the sane part of her was sensibly terrified of what they'd find when they located Kelly, and of what they were up against. She was even a little bit nervous of this tough woman who lived at a taco stand with her dog. "I only winter in Mexico," Harry had said. "I go where the work is in my RV."

They slowed, the quad's engine rattling roughly at lower RPMs. Lei peered around Harry; foothills loomed directly ahead, rendered in shades of gray, but Lei couldn't see any signs of civilization or life. No lights showed anywhere.

"Surprise is our only advantage." Harry pulled the ATV off the road and deep into the shadow of a boulder. Moonlight gleamed off Harry's bright teeth. "We will lose that if we roll up into the town on this noisy thing."

"We don't only have surprise. We also have a helluva lot of fire-power." Lei patted one of her Glocks. The cargo pockets of her pants were filled with spare clips, and a shotgun made a hard lump against her back under the backpack. Kona hopped out of his carrier. He whimpered with excitement from Harry's side.

"They may not have been armed when they took you, but I guarantee they are now. I hope you feel up to a run."

"Running is one of the things I do best." Lei was rested, hydrated, and her stomach was full of excellent food. She felt ready to take on an army.

They jogged down the moonlit ribbon of road, Kona a bulky dark shadow beside them. Lei strained her ears for any sounds of danger, but heard nothing but a faraway coyote howl, the soft desert wind in the brush, and the cry of a night bird.

She settled into a ground-eating lope, the weight of weapons unfamiliar but welcome. Fifteen or twenty minutes went by as she breathed easily. The woman beside her never slowed, nor did her respiration speed up. Remembering the firmness of Harry's waist, the solidity of her shoulder, Harry *was* stronger. Apparently, all Harry did down in Mexico was train all day, and it showed. The only thing better than going in with Harry would be if Harry's trainer, the mysterious Cruz with his combat skills, would somehow read their minds and join the party.

A series of abandoned buildings loomed ahead, hunched black shapes in a landscape rendered in shades of gray.

"The mining town," Harry whispered. "We should take cover in case they have anyone watching."

They trotted into the shadow of a derelict store, its broken sign worn beyond readability even in daylight.

"I don't see anyone. No cars, nothing," Lei said. Urgency to reach her friend beat in her veins. "Let's just find them."

She moved past Harry back out into the open, pulling one of the Glocks and holding it in low ready position as she jogged down the middle of the road between the buildings, scanning from side to side for any sight of human habitation or danger.

Kona's sharp bark was the only warning she had.

CHAPTER SEVEN

A DARK SHADOW streaked toward her, and Lei spun in a crouch, Glock trained on the threat—and the jackrabbit bounded past, raising tiny puffs of dust in its wake. Lei lowered the gun. "Crap."

"You almost shot our element of surprise." Harry's voice came from over her shoulder. Lei hadn't heard her approach. "Get behind me. You're going to blow this for us."

Chastened, Lei fell in behind the more experienced Harry, and they moved silently to the cover of the abandoned buildings. Kona, at Harry's side, lolled his tongue at Lei in a doggy grin, as if sympathizing. If she got out of this, she was getting a dog. Something big and fierce, but loving—like Kona. Aunty's idea seemed like a good one, now that she'd met the German Shepherd.

Harry led them from building to building, keeping to the shadows —but there was nothing to see but the occasional tumbleweed, trying to trip them, nothing to hear but a far-off hoot owl. They reached the end of the stretch of buildings.

"Now what?" Lei's voice was a harsh whisper.

"They must be up by the mine."

Lei adjusted the straps of the backpack carrying extra weapons that rubbed harshly against her sweating shoulders. The equipment inside made a metallic clank, and suddenly, far up ahead, they heard a deep, bellowing bark.

"Found them," Harry said. She pulled her weapon, a silenced SIG, and loped down the last bit of battered road toward a mound of rock outcroppings. Lei could see a gaping black cave in the front, and behind it, a small collection of buildings. Light seeped around closed doors and windows of one of the buildings ahead.

Lei's heart hammered, but she concentrated on controlling her breathing, imagining herself as the trained cop she wanted to be, cool and collected, on a raid. She stayed behind Harry, who made a gesture to Kona. The dog streaked off into the darkness as they left the road, taking to the scrub to approach the building from well behind in the darkness.

The dog near the building stopped barking, thankfully. Harry licked a finger and held it up, checking for the direction of the wind. The tiniest breeze rattled the seed-laden, dry skeletons of tumble-weeds, and she gave a brief nod and changed direction a little, Lei riding her wake.

The building was old, as all of these seemed to be, exuding a smell of dust, decay, and hopelessness. Inside, all was silent. The light flickered, probably a flame-lit lantern. Lei pressed into the black shadow of the building, and felt splintery wood beneath her skin.

Harry crept up to a boarded-up window. Orangey, flickering light shone from around its sill. She moved to the other side of the window so Lei could peek in through a crack as well.

It was hard to see what was going on inside the room with dust so thick on the pane. Lei rubbed a tiny hole in the dirt on the glass and applied her eye.

A kerosene lantern, turned down, sat on a rough wooden picnic table. Around the room, on the floor, were the lumpy dark shapes of sleeping people.

Lei looked frantically for Kelly, and finally spotted her by the shine of light on her long tangled hair, protruding from beneath a rough Mexican blanket.

Harry caught Lei's eye, gesturing toward a ladder lying on the ground on the side of the building. With her fingers, she indicated she was going up on the roof, where a round metal vent protruded. Lei was to go to the front door of the building and access it there.

"Where's Kona?" Lei whispered. Her voice sounded too loud, raspy as a summer cicada in the eerie night.

Harry gave a brief headshake, not explaining—but clearly the dog had some sort of role. Harry raised her brows in question about their rudimentary plan.

Lei nodded. As a strategy it was sketchy as hell, but Lei didn't have any better ideas.

Harry picked up the ladder, and Lei helped stabilize the broken, splintery structure against the old building as her partner climbed carefully, setting each foot gingerly on the brittle struts. Several were missing.

Harry made it to the flat expanse of roof, and Lei sighed with relief, wondering if the termite-riddled expanse would hold the other woman's weight. Harry gestured impatiently for Lei to move out, and, trembling with adrenaline, breath harsh in her lungs, Lei sidled toward the front of the building.

The main door was closed, a broad expanse of newer wood whose hinges looked sturdy by the light of the moon. The kidnappers had replaced whatever had been there before, not good news.

But the men hadn't posted a guard. Lei pulled her gun and positioned herself in front of the door, getting ready to try to kick it open.

She saw the dog at the same time as it spotted her.

They *had* posted a guard.

The big black shadow erupted from its shelter under a bush, barking like a hellhound as it hurled itself toward her.

Lei spun, aiming her weapon at the creature—but Kona got in the way, streaking in from the side and leaping on the other beast in a flurry of snarling and snapping.

Lei only had a moment to get through the door, before everyone was awake. She grabbed the handle and twisted. The portal opened, and Lei cranked the handle, hit the door with her shoulder, and leapt into the room.

Three men on the ground were throwing off blankets and fumbling for their weapons.

"Hands in the air," Lei yelled, pointing her Glock at the bald man who'd risen, gleaming head identifying him as Fernando. "*Los manos!* Up!"

"Come back to party, little girl?" said a voice from her left. Lei glanced quickly at Joao, greasy hair mussed with sleep. "And just when we were getting tired of your friend."

Kelly raised her head from the far corner of the room. Her mouth was taped, and her eyes looked like holes in the dim light.

Lei gritted her teeth in a snarl. "Hands up!"

Fernando had something in his hand. Lei couldn't tell what it was, but the other man, on her right, had stood up too. He also held a weapon.

"Drop it!" Lei barked, as loudly and authoritatively as she could, but she'd never aimed a gun at another human before, let alone pulled the trigger. Her stomach roiled with panic. Her hands trembled, holding the Glock; her fingers were not obeying her mental order to fire.

Joao leaned over, reaching for the rifle at his feet as Fernando took a long step toward Lei. Lei recognized the shape in his hand— the giant Buck knife she was already familiar with. His teeth shone in a grin, and a trick of the light made them look pointed.

Where the hell was Harry?

A gunshot boomed in the enclosed space, so loud it seemed to explode Lei's eardrums, and the unknown man on her right went down, a giant hole in his chest. Joao spun toward the sound, the rifle in his hands. Harry peered down through the hole where the rusted vent had been, holding a shotgun.

Lei shot Joao in the side as he raised the rifle and aimed for Harry.

The recoil of the handgun vibrated through her arms; the sound of the report much louder than she was prepared for. The expended brass flew up and hit her in the forehead, causing her next shot to go wide.

And she'd taken her eyes off Fernando.

The burly bald man hit her like a linebacker, bearing her backward to slam against the wall beside the door. His knife was at her throat, his teeth bared in a fierce grin as he pinned her against the wall.

"I've got you now, *chica,*" he breathed in her face, his breath foul.

Lei writhed beneath his heavy body, panic swamping her in a dark wave. Her vision telescoped. Her weapon dropped from nerveless fingers as he squeezed her wrist in a meaty grip. She twisted in Fernando's grasp, breathless from the force of the impact.

Lei's mind flew away to that dark place where it went when things were just too terrible to know. This man wasn't the first to hold her down and touch her in unspeakable ways.

One moment Fernando was there, crushing her as her vision narrowed to a black dot. The next, Fernando's head was gone, flying off his shoulders to land on the ground with a wet thump that sounded like a dropped melon.

Lei was bathed in hot, jetting blood as the man's corpse, not yet knowing it was dead, leaned heavily on her, twitching. She pushed against it, and the body fell away, landing beside its head.

Lei didn't feel the blood soaking her clothing, spattered across her face. She didn't feel anything in the place she'd retreated to. But her eyes were strained, and when she blinked, they stung, and she could feel the blood cooling on her face.

"You injured?" Harry asked. The sword she held dripped onto the dirt floor.

"No." Lei bent and picked the Glock up off the ground. She

walked past the bodies to Kelly, squatting beside where her friend lay on a pallet. She pulled Joao's knife from the scabbard at her waist and cut Kelly's duct tape bindings. She carefully peeled the sticky silver tape from Kelly's mouth. "You okay?"

"I am now," Kelly said. "You look really, really gross."

Lei laughed, and the sound of her harsh chuckle sucked her back into her body. She stood, trembling with the aftermath, and looked over to see Harry finish off Joao with a matter-of-fact stab to the back as the man crawled toward the fallen rifle.

Lei stumbled a few feet away and upchucked against the wall.

Kona nosed through the door. The dog's muzzle was streaked with blood and he was limping, but he was clearly the victor of the tussle in front of the building.

Lei wiped her mouth on her blood-speckled shoulder. She had to breathe through another wave of nausea. She looked back at her friend. "Are you sure you're okay, Kelly?"

Kelly had removed the last of the tape and she tossed off the Mexican blanket and stood up, brushing herself down vigorously, as if to get rid of every dirty thing that had touched her.

"I got groped and I had to give everybody a couple of blowjobs, but Fernando didn't let them rape me. Said they'd get more money from my parents if I wasn't damaged. They contacted my folks this afternoon and sent them pictures. I think the money was going to be on its way tomorrow."

"You got lucky, then." Harry wiped the long gleaming blade of the sword on Joao's shirt before sheathing it. "Let's get out of here and destroy the evidence."

"How?" Lei gestured to the three fallen bodies.

"We'll fire the place." Harry said. "I've done this before, so listen up. We need to make sure there's nothing identifying on these bodies."

"Wait. There's a baby," Kelly said.

Lei and Harry froze, staring at her. "A what?" Harry said.

Just then, a thin wail came from the corner of the room.

CHAPTER EIGHT

Lei froze. "That sounds like a baby."

"It *is* a baby." Kelly covered her face with her hands. "Poor thing."

"Why is it here?" Harry was already heading for the corner of the room, where a crude curtain cut off the area.

"I think—they had another captive and—she died and left that baby. They were pissed about it. From what I could gather, these guys capture women and sell them to whorehouses," Kelly said. "They were trying to find a buyer for the baby."

Harry swore and spat on the ground, then slipped behind the curtain. The crying stopped. Apparently, Harry knew how to calm the creature. Lei was thankful; babies terrified her.

She made herself reach into Joao's pockets, looking for anything identifying. She had to master fear and revulsion and truly experience that this man couldn't hurt her, that he was done and dead.

Lei found the keys to the men's truck. A silver cross and a rabbit's foot dangled off the key ring, giving Lei a twinge for the first time—Joao, whoever he'd been, was dead now because of her. She shook it off, noticing the Mustang's key among the others.

"Let's get your car back, Kelly." She held up the keys.

"And here's some extra kerosene." Kelly held up a square gallon container of the piney-smelling accelerant she'd found in the corner. "Should I scatter it around?"

"Hang on a minute." Harry emerged from behind the curtain. She held an impossibly small, swaddled bundle to her shoulder. "You didn't tell us the baby was an infant girl."

"How would I know?" Kelly said crossly. "I never saw it. They'd go back behind the curtain and do stuff to it when it cried."

"Well, this baby's only a few weeks old." Harry carefully lowered the child so they could see a tiny round face, and the tuft of dark hair protruding from her wrappings. "She was wet, so I changed her, that's why she was crying. We'll have to take her with us. Fortunately, all the baby's stuff is back there, too."

"Oh wow," Lei breathed. "How are we going to explain a baby?"

"You two won't have to explain anything," Harry snapped. "I'll take care of her for the moment and figure something out. Lei, finish searching the bodies. Kelly, go pack up the baby's stuff and find a bag or something to put it in, while I get her settled in the car." Kona rejoined his mistress and they headed for the door.

Lei gulped as she rolled Fernando's head into position near his shoulders with her toe. The man's eyes were open, and surprise was frozen on his face forever. "We will have to destroy as much of this building and these bodies as we can."

"Absolutely." Kelly had pushed the curtain aside and was thrusting baby stuff into a canvas grocery sack.

Lei removed Fernando's wallet, emptied money and his ID from it, and dropped it back on his body. She moved on to the next man. "Let's try to make this look like an accident. It will save hassles later if no one's looking for a killer."

"It's a stretch that anyone'd believe this is an accident," Kelly said, emerging with the bulging bag. "I'll go find Harry."

Lei tossed her the keys. "In case you need to unlock the car."

Kelly nodded and exited.

Lei put her hands on her hips and looked around the chaotic

scene, trying to remember what she'd been studying about forensic investigation. "The bodies need to look natural," she muttered. "And the cause of death needs to be obvious and plausible."

She dragged Joao's body by the heels back to his pallet, covering him with his blanket. "Hopefully it seems like the lamp fell over and started a fire."

She didn't want to move Fernando's body back to his pallet, so she dragged that over near him and positioned his body onto it, then made sure his head was centered above it and covered the whole business with a blanket.

Harry and Kelly reappeared. "The baby's settled in a box in the back seat of the Mustang, and Kona is keeping an eye on her," Harry said. She assessed the room with a quick glance. "Good job, Lei. These poor innocent men were victims of a fallen lamp."

"Just what I was thinking," Lei said.

They staged the room as best they could, and Kelly poured the kerosene she'd found over the wooden table in the center. When they were ready and the bodies positioned, Harry used her shotgun to tip over the lit lamp into the pool of fuel.

The table caught fire with a whump.

Kerosene didn't have the explosive quality of gasoline, so they had plenty of time to retrieve Kelly's purse and Lei's backpack from the corner where the men had thrown them and shut the door of the building. Harry fiddled with the lock on the front door and jammed it. Inside, the fire crackled merrily, flames growing to reach up and touch the tinder-dry ceiling beams.

They were still unfastening the Mustang's bumper from the winch on the back of the truck when the whole building caught fire.

Grunting with effort, wriggling through the dust, Lei disconnected the steel hook from the undercarriage of the car. She backed out on her belly and stood up. She dusted herself off, but dirt clung to the blood soaking her garments in a sticky paste.

Harry had hauled the dog Kona had killed into the doorway of the burning building, and the animal's body caught fire with a burnt hair smell. The three women watched the leaping flames consume the remains of the violent scene.

"Do you want to take the truck, too?" Lei brushed vainly at the filth coating her. Kelly, meanwhile, got into the Mustang and turned it on. The powerful engine caught with a roar.

"No. Let's leave the truck and its keys here. With any luck at all, this looks like these guys were partying and passed out when their kerosene lamp fell over, causing a tragic accident. You two can drop me by the quad and go on your way," Harry said.

"I don't know how you're going to carry a baby on the quad," Lei said.

"I have the carrying rack on the back. Her box will fit there just fine." Harry seemed to have taken full control of the infant and didn't want to let it out of her sight; and that was fine with Lei.

Lei went to the truck's cab. She wiped Fernando's keys off with a bit of greasy rag she found in the truck. She wiped down the seats and window jambs too, removing Kelly's prints. She checked carefully for any evidence, retrieving one of Kelly's flowered sandals from the truck's floor. Their crude doctoring of the scene wouldn't fool any good investigator, but one could hope the cops wouldn't look too closely at the convenient death of these undesirables.

Lei dropped the keys on the floor of the truck, searching the ground for Kelly's other sandal. She found it on the way to the burning building.

"We better get going," Harry called. "This fire's going to attract some attention, even out here."

"Coming." Lei jogged back to the Mustang. Harry sat in the back seat, on one side of the baby's box; Kona sat on the other side. Lei jumped into the passenger seat in front and buckled her seatbelt. She waggled the sandals. "I found your shoes, Kelly."

"Good. I don't like going barefoot." Kelly hit the gas, spinning the convertible into a tight turn to drive away from the pyre they'd ignited.

Lei hadn't expected that her first time at a crime scene would be on the wrong side of the law—and it didn't feel good. She didn't want to have to carry any more secrets than she already did. She wanted to fight crime legitimately, in the clear light of day, not in darkness with weapons with their serial numbers filed off.

This kind of crime fighting wasn't her thing—but she couldn't deny that Harry's idea had worked. They'd done what they had to do; Kelly was safe now, and so was a tiny, innocent baby.

Kona put his head between the seat and the doorjamb and nuzzled Lei's hair. He licked blood off her shoulder as the Mustang accelerated on the long, dusty road back to civilization.

CHAPTER NINE

LEI STRETCHED out on a lounge chair beside the pool, fighting a sense of unreality as Kelly handed her the tanning lotion. "I wish you'd buy a better suit. You have a great figure, but you look like my grandma in that." Her friend gestured to Lei's no-nonsense, high-cut tank.

"You're showing enough for both of us," Lei said, gesturing to the skimpy white bikini that made the most of Kelly's curves. Kelly blinked at the sharp comment and dropped the tanning oil onto Lei's stomach.

Harry, face down on her lounger, looked up. The string of her top was untied, baring her sleek brown back. Her amber-brown eyes were tired. "Be nice, girls."

Last night they'd reached the boulder where Harry had stashed the quad, and after a discussion involving the filth coating Lei, the money they'd spent on the resort, and the importance of pretending everything was normal, the trio, including dog and baby, had returned to Harry's RV together and everyone cleaned up as best they could.

"Please come with us to the resort," Kelly begged Harry. "I know it won't be a problem to add a room for you. Let me pay. It's the least I can do to thank you for rescuing me."

Harry, looking down at her grubby jeans, nodded. "I'll come for a couple of days, if they'll take Kona. Would be nice to have a long hot shower and a real bed, and we can figure out what to do about the baby."

Bringing Kona into the resort had cost a small fortune, but Kelly's parents, relieved she'd "escaped," as Kelly put it, were happy to put the whole thing on their gold Mastercard when Kelly got done explaining, leaving out the dead bodies in a burnt building. They'd insisted Lei and Kelly stay in Mexico and drive back to the Bay Area after a few days of relaxation in the hotel. "We came for a vacation and we need one now, more than ever," Kelly had told her parents, and she got her way as she always did.

The girls had checked into the hotel in Cabo San Lucas the night before. Now, Lei glanced over at Harry. The baby girl was napping in the shade in a respectable portable bassinet they'd picked up, but judging by the circles under her eyes, Harry had lost sleep last night caring for the infant.

"I need a drink." Lei waved for a waiter. They ordered a round of mojitos. Kelly pulled the brim of her large white sombrero down firmly, blocking Lei from her view.

Lei poured some of the oil into her hand, massaging it onto her legs. It was only twenty-four hours since their raid, but it felt like it had happened a lifetime ago. Still, intrusive images from the night kept flashing in front of her eyes, making this idyllic setting feel like a dream, and she hadn't slept well either. "I'm sorry, Kelly. I'm . . . having trouble just brushing everything off. Moving on."

"It's okay. Me, too," Kelly said, plucking at the knot of her skimpy bikini. "I feel so weird, like any minute the cops are going to charge in and bust us."

The drinks arrived just then, and there was a flurry of distraction. Finally, the three sat forward and clinked brightly colored, umbrella-decorated glasses filled with frosty drinks.

"To freedom," Harry said.

"To escaping," Kelly said.

"To the sword," Lei said.

They laughed, nervous giggles with darting glances, but no one was near their spot at the free-form pool, turquoise as a gem in the midday sun. Lei sat back and sipped her mojito, gazing unseeing at the pool.

Her body was sore from the struggles of the night before, with bruises marring her legs, arms and shoulders, and her muscles were stiff from running with the backpack of gear they hadn't used. Gradually the combination of alcohol, warmth, and a sense of safety relaxed her, and her eyes grew heavy. She set the empty glass down, rolled over, and fell asleep.

Someone was coming. A hand was grabbing her.

Lei started, awakening with a cry.

"Lei. Your shoulders are getting burned. Let's cool off." Kelly pulled back from touching Lei, clearly concerned by her jerky overreaction.

Lei sat up and swung her legs to the side. "You said you did something like last night before," she told Harry. "How do you just move on from it?"

Harry eyed Lei from where she sat on a lounger, holding the infant on her lap with a bottle tilted to the baby's lips. "Meditation helps. And working out. Cruz says training the mind is as important as training the body."

"I don't really know how to do either." Lei stood up, tugging her tank suit into place. With her history, she didn't feel comfortable uncovered—body self-confidence was one more thing Charlie Kwon had stolen from her.

She couldn't remember most of what her mother's boyfriend had done to her; it only came in bits and flashes, but that was just as well. She didn't want to remember; she just wanted to be free of it.

Around the pool area, several college-aged men were sunning, drinking, and shooting pool at a nearby table, obviously here for the same kind of fun they were. Granny suit or not, Kelly wasn't the only one getting looks. One of the guys raised his drink to her with a smile, and Lei made herself smile back.

"Shake it off," Lei muttered. "Murder was yesterday. Today we party." She dove into the pool and drowned her troubled thoughts.

"This is going to make your eyes really pop. They're such an unusual color." Harry tipped her face up obediently and let Kelly daub glittery purple shadow on her eyelids.

"Eyes popping doesn't seem a very good thing," Harry said drily. "I can get a guy to do that, but it usually involves a chokehold."

Lei, whisking on mascara, almost stabbed herself in the eye with the wand. "I can imagine that too well."

"You two need to allow your inner goddesses out to play. You're way too serious. I tell Lei that all the time. At least you agreed to wear my dress, Lei."

"What there is of it! I had more coverage in my bathing suit." Lei looked ruefully down at the sleeveless tube of black stretch material that covered her from breasts to crotch, and not much farther. She wriggled her breasts a little deeper into the dress, but that made the skirt come up higher, cupping her bottom. She wasn't sure which to let hang out. "I look like a hooker." Lei viewed herself in the mirror. Her legs were tanned and endless in tall Lucite heels she'd planned to wear with a much more conservative garment.

"If you don't get some action tonight, I'll eat my hat." Kelly gestured to the discarded sombrero, hanging off the corner of the chair. "And it's big."

Clearly Kelly was determined to resume her life as if that stretch of rough road that ended in murder and fire had never happened.

Harry glanced at the door, a line between her dark brows. "I hope the baby is okay with that hotel sitter."

"Be careful. You're getting awfully attached to it," Lei cautioned, worried for her new friend.

Harry frowned. "She's not an 'it,' she's a beautiful little girl." Both women turned to stare at Harry, who looked drop-dead gorgeous in a sleek silvery dress of Kelly's. Harry glared right back at them. "She's special."

"Um. Okay. But that special child's an orphaned Mexican citizen with no name," Kelly said. "You can't just keep her, Harry. She's not a puppy."

Harry looked away, glowering. "Let's just go, already."

The three of them linked arms and went down to the dance floor: Lei all in black, Kelly in red, and Harry shining in silver. Pulsing retro eighties music was easy to get moving to after a few drinks. Determined to shake off their brush with death, Lei began to relax and have fun as the three of them got moving on the dance floor. Within minutes, guys moved in to dance with them.

Lei smiled at the blond, blue-eyed surfer dude who did a hilarious chicken dance in front of her. Clearly, he wasn't someone who took himself too seriously, and he was easy on the eyes, with a mop of salty-looking curls and a lot of nice tan muscle.

"You've got interesting moves," she laughed. Lei glanced over at Harry. Her new friend was doing some dirty dancing with a tall, dark, and handsome man, while Kelly was handling two guys with no trouble at all.

This was the vacation they'd come for. Surfer Dude wasn't her type, but maybe with enough tequila . . .

"I need another drink!" Lei hollered to her dance partner across the techno-pop blaring from the loudspeakers.

"Let me buy it for you!" Surfer Dude hollered back. He took her hand and towed her through packed, gyrating bodies toward the bar. He elbowed a space for them and ordered her a Sex on the Beach.

Lei pushed him in the chest. "Hoping to get lucky, I see."

"Funny you should say that. That's what people call me." His blue eyes crinkled with good humor. "All the best surfers have nicknames."

"Lucky? Really?" Lei quirked a brow.

"Yeah. I'm Lucky. But you can call me anything you want, babe."

Their drinks arrived. Lei picked hers up. It was frothy, peachy, and refreshing. "Mmm, nice choice. I think I like getting Lucky." She smiled, pleased with the play on words.

"And what do I call you?"

"Lei."

He frowned. "Lay? You mean you're easy? Am I going to be charged by the hour?" His good humor disappeared as his glance raked her outfit.

"Oh no." Lei choked on her drink and set it down. "No. No. My name is Lei. L-E-I. It's Hawaiian."

Now he laughed, smacking his forehead in exaggerated relief. "Holy crap. Lei gets Lucky. You can't make this stuff up."

They finished their drinks, making easy conversation. Lei's head spun a little, but in a good way, as he towed her back on the dance floor.

A few more drinks and songs later, Lucky leaned in to speak in her ear. "Let's get out of here to somewhere quieter." He took Lei's hand, towing her toward glass sliders that opened onto the pool deck.

Lei glanced back; she'd really rather dance some more, but her friends were fully occupied with their partners on the floor. And this was what she'd come for—a good time, and after all, his name was Lucky.

They emerged from the dance area into much cooler air on the deck surrounding the pool. Tiny lights crisscrossed the area, strung on lines from the corners of the buildings. A memory of the burning mine building and all it contained flashed across Lei's mind, and horror made her trip in her high heels. Lucky looped an arm around her waist and pulled her close.

"Careful. Don't want to have you swimming in the pool in those awesome shoes." He seemed to have a destination in mind. Quelling her anxiety, Lei let him pull her along. Down and away from the pool, they reached an isolated cabana with a canvas roof and sides, the curtains looped back from a soft mattress piled high with pillows.

"Wow. You knew just where this was." Lei glanced around nervously. "We're all alone out here."

"Relax. We're just going to have some fun. Spooky little thing, aren't you?" Lucky sat on the edge of the cabana bed, his white teeth a flash in the dim light. "Come here." He pulled her between his legs, his hands at her waist.

Lei lost her balance in the heels she wasn't used to, and fell forward across him, sprawling gracelessly over his body and knocking him backward.

"Oh wow! I'm so sorry!" she gasped.

He tightened his arms around her. "Got you just where I want you."

He kissed her, bold and invasive. Lei tried to stay with the kiss, in her body, experiencing this, but immediately she went to that other place, somewhere high above the cabana. She could see herself below, passive in the blond man's grasp, her arms around him, her mouth kissing him back—but it was happening to someone else.

His hand slid up her leg, under the impossibly short skirt, and gripped the round of her buttock. He squeezed and caressed her.

"I love your ass," he said against her mouth. "You're so tight. I can't wait to be in you."

He was moving way too fast, but it was more than that.

"No," Lei said.

This was wrong.

He wasn't the right man, and this wasn't the right place or time.

"What are you talking about? You're my Lucky Lay," he murmured, nibbling her neck, grinding her pelvis against his.

"No." Lei pushed at Lucky more forcefully. "I don't want to do this."

"Cock tease!" His hands were like an octopus, crawling over her body, invading, burning her skin with their intimacy. "You dress like this and think you can say no? How much will it be? I'll pay if that's what you want."

"No! Let go!" Lei thrashed. She couldn't believe this was happening. He'd seemed so nice. She bucked and resisted, but he'd pinned her down by the arms. "No!"

"I believe the lady said no," a low masculine voice said from behind them. Lucky, panting, turned his head. From beneath him, Lei could see a shadowy figure—and there was coiled menace in his stance.

Lucky let go of Lei and rolled to the side. "Sorry about the misunderstanding. We had a crossed wire." He stood up. "See you back on the dance floor." He walked rapidly away.

Clearly, something about the man looking down at them had spooked him.

Lei sat up, straightening her skimpy top and pulling down her skirt as far as it would go—that dilemma again. She leaned forward, unbuckling the ridiculous shoes, letting her rumpled curls fall forward to hide her face.

She'd almost been assaulted again, in a fairly public place, and some stranger had to rescue her. What a disaster. Some cop she was going to be, if the police academy would even have her . . .

The backlit man advanced to stand in front of Lei, his legs slightly apart, arms loose at his sides. "Did he hurt you?" His voice was silk over steel and raised the hairs on Lei's arms.

She stood up with the shoes dangling from one hand. "Just my pride."

Now she could see what he looked like, as light fell on the man's face. His eyes were liquid chocolate, with lashes any woman would envy. His hair lay in tight coils against his head like a lamb's; his skin was golden brown. He was dressed for action in a black tank top, cargo pants, and combat boots.

"You're Cruz," Lei said. "Harry's trainer."

"I am." They took each other's measure for a long moment. He smiled. "I see why Harry likes you."

"Harry likes me?"

"Yes. She asked me to come meet you. Asked me to work with you a little."

"Really?" Lei's tongue was too thick for her mouth as she stared at Cruz, spellbound by his beauty, by the leashed power of him, by the serenity he emanated. How could she be so thoroughly smitten when she'd almost just been raped? Lei took a step back, away from him, and the feel of the cool gritty cement beneath her bare feet anchored her.

This must be some bizarre reaction. Her therapist back in San Rafael probably had a name for such a thing. "Harry must have seen that I wasn't handling the stress from last night very well."

"Yes. There are some techniques I can show you." Cruz bent down, a supple movement, and picked up a small granite pebble from a nearby potted palm. "Put out your hand."

Nervously, Lei extended her hand, palm up. He dropped the stone, still warm from the sunny day, into her hand and curled her fingers over it. His touch was light and confident, and over too quickly. "Carry that with you. Rub it when you're worried. Put your fear and negative feelings into the stone. It will carry them for you."

Lei looked down at the pebble in her hand. "It's not magic. It's just a rock from a planter."

"It's what you think it is. And for you, it needs to be a container. Come with me."

Lei, carrying her shoes, followed him into the darkness without question.

53

CHAPTER TEN

CRUZ LED Lei away from the lighted area of the resort, heading down a graveled path past bungalows set in a row to the beach. The moon was high and full, as it had been the previous nights. The long, curving stretch of beach, marked at one end with cliffs and the famous stone arch the area was known for, was bathed in silvery light.

The sand and moonlight reminded Lei of their raid, and her heart sped up. She rubbed the pebble in her hand, testing what Cruz had told her to do—picturing her fears flowing down her nerves and filling the stone, which expanded to hold whatever she sent it.

Here she was, following yet another strange man into the dark—but this time, her feelings were vastly different. Cruz was here to teach her something, to heal something in her that had been wounded, and even without the things Harry had said about him, she instinctively trusted him.

They fell in step as they walked along the beach. Lights and music from the resorts leaked down to meld with the soft surge of the surf, speckled with the glow of bioluminescence, a magical sight. As they walked, Lei felt her heart rate lowering.

She was safe in Cruz's company. Harry had called him for her, and he was going to help her let go of the aftereffects of the raid. Perhaps even the humiliation of Lucky's crude assault. Maybe he could even help with the scars Kwon had left on her—though that seemed like a ridiculous hope.

They reached the far end of the beach, bordered in cliffs, a long way from any other human presence.

"Put your shoes down."

Lei did.

Cruz led them to the damp, hard-packed sand near the water's edge. "We're going to do a moving meditation. I want you to concentrate on being in your body and the sensations of it moving through space. Harry tells me you do *taekwondo*. This is different. It's called *tai chi*."

"Okay."

Lei stood behind Cruz as he faced the calm, moonlit sea. She breathed deeply and slowly as she imitated the trainer's strong, slow, sweeping movements, deliberate and centered, even down to swirling kicks and turns. More and more as time slipped past, Lei's mind went still, her soul settling into the center of her body.

They moved silently in the darkness in an elegant dance for a timeless hour, and finally Cruz came to a stop. He turned to her, placing his hands palms together at chest height. She did so as well.

They bowed to each other.

Lei felt warm and loose, her extremities prickling. She was gloriously alive, her bruises forgotten. "Thank you," she whispered.

"You can do this any time you need to come back into your body." He reached out and took her hand, and she had a sense he seldom did such a thing. "There is another healing I have for you. If you are willing to take a chance."

The blood rushed to her face; her lips tingled as if he'd kissed her. Who was this mysterious moonlit man? Had God sent him, or something darker? It didn't matter. However he had appeared, she desperately needed whatever he had for her.

"Please," she breathed.

Cruz led her up from the water's edge into the deep purple shadow of the cliffs. "We begin by getting in touch with each other's body rhythms and breathing. Just follow what I do, as you did before."

He stepped forward to stand very close. His breath, smelling slightly of cloves, warmed her face. His body, only a foot or two away, was slightly musky, and she felt the heat of him. Slowly, deliberately, he circled an arm around her and set a hand, fingers spread, on her back at the base of her spine.

The other hand he set on her chest, between her breasts.

Lei's pulse quickened with familiar fear. She gazed into the dark of his extraordinary eyes and breathed slowly, calming herself.

She stretched out a hand and set it in the deep curve of his back, where the swell of his firm, round buttocks began. The other hand she set in the middle of the hard wall of his chest, a mirror of how he held her.

They gazed into each other's eyes. Their breathing fell into sync.

A tiny wind stirred their hair to brush over each other like fragile antennae. The moon made silvery gleams over Cruz's profile, gilding along his forehead and nose.

Lei's mind leaped into overdrive—she was touching a stranger, rather intimately, in an isolated place.

She focused on what was happening in the moment, trying to stay present. In her partner's steady gaze, she saw nothing but compassion, and yes, attraction and appreciation, but not the kind of lust that took all and gave nothing.

Cruz's eyes, his body, held something different.

He was very warm beneath her hands, springy almost. Her fingertips moved slightly to explore the sensation of his skin through the thin shroud of his clothing, and she felt his fingers move slightly as well, imitating her.

As the moments unspooled, Lei was still in her body, and she was enjoying the feeling of his closeness, of the way their breath was shared, the matching of their pulses.

She was with a man, touching him, he touching her, and she hadn't gone to that other place. This was the first time she'd stayed present for this long.

Lei felt a smile move over her face, and he echoed it, his teeth shining like pearls in the moonlight, strung perfectly along the frame of his jaw.

She seldom thought poetic things like that.

Lei took a tiny step closer toward him, and Cruz to her.

Now their hands on each other's chests were pressed tight between their bodies.

Cruz spread the fingers of the hand on her back and massaged and explored her waist. Lei shut her eyes, and she could feel how she was to him through his hand: firm yet soft, her back a pleasing curve as he pulled her closer.

She did the same, spreading her fingers to draw him as close as she could. His pelvis was slightly higher than hers since he was a few inches taller, and the curve of her belly fit against his abdomen like two parts of a puzzle. His back was hard beneath her hand, the muscles corded ridges, different from her lithe curves.

His heartbeat picked up beneath her hand, his breath flowing slightly faster.

She was grateful to be looking into his kind, dark eyes as she felt her own arousal, an unfamiliar throb, almost a pain, between her legs. She could feel him too, a thickening at their joined hips. She could almost see their blood heating in the darkness.

Arousal was an unfamiliar, slightly scary sensation. She'd lost that feeling to Kwon, when she was just a child, and it had never visited her so strongly before.

Cruz lowered himself slowly, and she followed. He sat cross-legged in the sand, and using his hands, he showed her that she was to sit on his lap, facing him, her legs over his, their bellies touching. "This is called the *yam yub*," he whispered, his voice husky. "A sacred position."

Her former stiffness and clumsiness gone, Lei sank into his lap.

The tight confines of the tubelike spandex dress felt binding and ridiculous, so she peeled it up.

Cruz helped, lifting the garment off her head. She wasn't wearing a bra, and her breasts sprang free and peaked in the cool night air as she breathed deep in relief, dropping the garment. Moonlight shone on the pale rounds of her chest. Cruz's eyes traveled over her, lingering there a moment, before they returned to hers.

In his gaze she saw anticipation, and delight in her beauty. Nothing more. Nothing that felt intrusive or demanding. Nothing that required anything of her or would take anything from her that she didn't want to give. *You're beautiful*, his gaze said. *I want you, of course. But that is all it is.*

Lei reached for the edge of his shirt and eased it off, up over his head, baring his upper body as well, and she looked her fill at him.

He was sparely and beautifully made, perfectly proportioned in the way of an athlete who builds muscle from the practice of his art. His narrow waist flared up into a smooth, wide chest, his nipples were small dark coins, and his collarbones a visually pleasing rack from which the swell of his shoulder muscles rose. His neck was a column bisected by the fluttering of the pulse in his throat, and the tiniest wind off the water blew a black curl against the shell of his ear.

"Ah," she said. "You're beautiful."

"As are you," he breathed, and brought his arms down around her waist, drawing her close and tight, so that their pelvises touched. She embraced his shoulders. Their hips aligned, and their skin touched from waist to shoulder.

Lei expected the sex to begin, but it didn't.

Instead, he wriggled her intimately close, just holding her for several breaths, and gently, he rested his head on her shoulder. It felt heavy, a weight of trust.

Very carefully, she lowered her head to rest on his firm, meaty shoulder, too. She shut her eyes. She breathed with him, enjoying the friction of his hardness against her panties, the length of their touching skins, the perfect alignment of their hearts and breath.

She was still in her body.

The victory of it flushed her with a swirl of delicious feeling. His scent filled her nostrils, drugging and delicious. His heart rate jumped in response to hers, and their pulses thundered against each other—but there was no other movement.

She had to taste him.

Lei lifted her head just the slightest bit to lick the lobe of his ear. He shuddered beneath her as if struck by lightning.

He tasted so good: salty and nourishing, as if tasting him fed her.

She wanted more but restrained herself as he lifted his head and slowly, so slowly, licked the tiny wound Joao had made on her neck.

A thrill zipped through her and the feeling between her legs seemed to heat and pulse with her pounding heartbeat. She was burning, on fire, and only he could put it out. She wriggled impatiently and reached for the button on his pants.

"Settle," he breathed against her throat. "Stay in the moment. This is not like anything you've ever done before or will do again. This is all there is."

Was he telling her they wouldn't have sex?

Disappointment and frustration warred with a tiny flicker of relief—but regardless, Cruz was in charge. She struggled to accept his words, to restrain herself, to relax.

Gradually, she settled back into his embrace, and laid her head on his shoulder again. Their faces almost touched as they breathed each other's air. She was melting, spreading across his hard chest, over his shoulders, her body going boneless, a spill of warm honey puddling in his lap.

At last he moved—stroking his hands up her back, from her buttocks, up the base of her spine to her shoulders and back down again, kneading, pressing, and molding her against him. Slow, deliberate, deep, the sensation was exquisite, a seated massage. She could feel the edges of herself: under his hands she was slender, firm, and supple, as if he were creating her as he shaped her. Lei sighed, a deep sound of fulfillment, as he cupped her bottom in his hands.

Wanting to give back, Lei touched his head. She ran her hands and fingertips again and again through the soft tight curls of his hair, from the roots to the ends. His head fell back, his eyes shutting in pleasure, as, using only her fingertips, she massaged the precious sphere of his skull. She ran her hands over the smooth hard planes of his face, fingers brushing the sculpted mouth she longed to kiss—and back up into his scalp she went, digging her fingers into the pressure points on his head that an EMT friend of hers had shown her could bring relief from pain.

Goosebumps erupted all over him at her touch, and finally a groan of ecstasy escaped him. He wrapped both arms around her and crushed her close. That sound made her arch her back, pressing ever closer, his face almost between her breasts.

She couldn't help moving her hips against his hardness, craving more of that friction.

Cruz grasped her by the waist and pushed her back and away. Their bodies weren't touching at all now, but for her hands stabilizing herself at his shoulders and her legs over his. Lei whimpered at the loss of contact.

"Perhaps this is enough for tonight," he whispered.

Suddenly, Lei understood the violent response Lucky had had when denied. Lei wanted to bite Cruz—throw him down, work him over, to assault him and ride him until she found her release.

She wanted to rape him.

Lei settled deep in the well of his legs and looked him in the eyes again. "It's in me too," she whispered. "Rape. Violence."

"It's in all of us."

"Oh, Cruz. I'm sorry." Grief and shame swamped her, surging up from her toes in a wave of tears that broke over her and wrung a sob from her lips—and he kissed her on that sob, capturing the sound and tears in his mouth, transmuting them into something shared, an acknowledgement of their mere humanity.

He pulled her back into his lap and settled into kissing her. And it wasn't like any kiss she'd ever had—it began as a thorough exploration, curious and tender, almost clinical, as their lips and tongues ignited sensations that went off in their joined bodies in cascades of feeling that they shared and observed . . . And then, it was an extension of their matched conversation, something rising and falling with the sound of the waves behind them, gradually building, soaring, and taking different forms.

Cruz's arms swirled around her on his lap, and hers moved around his shoulders, back, and neck. Their mouths never parted.

Without warning, Lei felt something suddenly uncoiling within her, a spiraling delight. She froze in his arms, lifting her head in astonishment—stiffening, transfixed, suffused with the sensation of an exquisite pleasure.

The fierce feeling roared like a freight train up her spine and blew off the top of her head, shattering her in his arms.

Cruz held her tight. He captured her mouth and took her cries into his kiss and swallowed them, and she could feel them become fuel in the furnace of his passion. A second later she felt the full power of his detonation in her arms, and she held on for dear life, riding it out with him.

A long breathless moment passed. Spangles and darkness swirled behind her eyes.

Lei sagged, and so did he. Very slowly, they tipped over, still clasped in each other's arms, into the cool sand.

Lei rested her head on his chest. His thundering heart calmed beneath her ear and so did hers. Their heaving breaths slowed.

"Wow. What was that?" she whispered.

"The *kundalini*," he whispered back. "It's a coiled energy stored at the base of the spine. Only sometimes is it released in sex."

"Oh." Lei shut her eyes and floated on physical bliss.

Finally, Cruz sat up. "Let's go for a swim."

There was no embarrassment between them as they stripped out of their remaining clothing, never letting go of each other's hands, and walked down into the ocean.

The green and blue glitter of bioluminescence foamed in the gentle surf. Lei smiled as the water, so warm it reminded her of her childhood in Hawaii, swirled and rose around her body in a new set of exquisite sensations. She dove under the dark surface, opening her eyes in spite of the stinging to see the sparkles, still holding Cruz's hand. He followed, and they swam as long as they could underwater.

Out deeper, they let go, but continued their game of follow-and-lead as they swam, dove, and splashed in the glowing water. Cruz caught her hand and they moved in closer to shore, walking into waist-deep water. Their bodies touched, but there was none of the sexual fire of before—his presence felt friendly, companionable, like a trusted friend.

Gratitude rose up in Lei. "Cruz. Thank you." She tugged his hand and he turned to her. She touched wet, salty lips to his in a brief kiss. "You did something. A magic spell. I can be with someone now. I can love someone now. I'm different because of this."

"It was my honor," Cruz said formally. "He will be a very lucky man." He bowed to her in the same way he had when they finished their *tai chi.*

CHAPTER ELEVEN

Lᴇɪ ᴡᴏᴋᴇ ɢᴇɴᴛʟʏ to the sound of doves in the citrus tree outside her room, and the smell of orange blossoms. She stretched out on the hotel's luxurious sheets, sliding her naked body along the silky fabric. All of her nerve endings felt pleasantly abuzz with sensation, and she sighed, remembering Cruz walking her to her door, the soft kiss goodbye on her lips, the finger he then held to them as he winked one of those remarkable eyes.

Good. She didn't want to tell anyone about their encounter, either.

Getting up, Lei padded over to her laptop and turned it on. While that was booting up, she took a shower. She'd taken one last night too, just a brief rinse to get the salt off, but sleeping on her curly hair wet was never a good idea, and today was no exception.

A few minutes later, wearing one of the hotel's pristine terry cloth robes, she sat down in front of the computer and typed in 'kundalini.' Webster's defined the word as *"the yogic life force that is held to lie coiled at the base of the spine until it is aroused and sent to the head to trigger enlightenment."*

Lei smiled. She'd been enlightened, all right. She had a sense that everything they'd done had been part of some spiritual discipline that Cruz was well-versed in.

Lei surfed through the local news, looking for anything about the bodies and the burned building. Eventually she found a small article and dragged the main paragraph into a translation program: *"Three trespassers in the abandoned El Central Copper Mine were found burned in a kerosene accident involving alcohol. The public is reminded to stay away from private property."*

"Ha," Lei said aloud. "Yes." The day was getting better and better.

The phone rang by her bed and she picked it up. "Hello?"

"It's Harry. Come have coffee with me. Cruz has taken Kelly out for a crash course in self-defense, so the baby and I want company."

"Sure. Meet you by the pool?"

"Perfect." The woman hung up.

Lei looked at herself in the mirror. Her eyes were bright, her cheeks flushed, and with a little gel in her hair, her curls were behaving. She'd never looked better.

Something inside her had shifted—she was ready.

Ready to open her heart to someone—perhaps a dog. She smiled at that idea.

Lei dressed in the bikini Kelly had bought her when she purchased Harry's dress yesterday. She liked the sporty two-piece, cut high on the hip but more modest than the skimpy triangles Kelly was fond of. The bronzy color splashed with flowers complemented Lei's olive skin tone and brown locks. She tied the matching pareo around her hips, slid her feet into slippers, and left the room.

Harry was already in the pool, swimming laps with that fluid way she had of moving, and no one else was around yet. The baby lay peacefully in her carrier, gazing up at the tree overhead, a tiny fist that had escaped from her blanket waving. Kona, vigilant beside the carrier, got up to greet Lei with a nose to the crotch and a bump to her hand, asking for scritches.

A waiter came by, and Lei ordered a pot of coffee and some fruit for their table and made herself comfortable beside the child and the dog.

Why hadn't Harry done something about finding a placement for the baby? She frowned, concerned—surely someone was alive who knew about this child and would want her back!

She gazed down into the little girl's face. So sweet—the baby's eyes were round and brown under the tracery of her tiny brows, and her round cheeks seemed to press in on the plump rosebud of her mouth. She had straight black hair, a lot of it.

Lei glanced over at Harry's sleek dark head. Harry could easily pass as her mother, in looks at least.

No one else had joined them at the pool yet, so Lei stood up and began doing some of the slow, graceful movements she'd learned from Cruz last night. Kona, watching, lolled his tongue at her in a happy grin.

Harry swam to the side of the pool and grinned up at Lei. "Cruz taught you a few moves, I see."

A blush heated Lei's cheeks. She bent over to touch her toes, hiding it. "I'm sure I'm getting this whole *tai chi* thing wrong, but I want to learn. It seems like a great stress reliever, a moving meditation." She straightened up when she was fairly sure that her face had cooled. "I checked the news. Looks like the cops bought the cover story of an accidental fire."

Harry hoisted herself out of the pool with an easy boost of her toned arms. She shook her hair, spraying Lei playfully with droplets. "Told you they would. Lazy and corrupt can be a good thing at times. Let's have some coffee, then I'll show you a simple *tai chi* routine for daily use." Harry led Lei back to their loungers, where a thermal carafe had arrived and rested on a small table between cups, saucers, and bowls of fruit. "Man. It's going to be tough to go back to the RV after this."

"Kinda enjoying living like the one percent, myself. My aunt and I aren't anywhere in Kelly's economic bracket." Lei accepted the cup of coffee Harry handed her.

"So, how'd you girls meet?"

Lei filled her in. "I know we seem like an odd couple, but Kelly's good for me—and I think I'm good for her, too."

"After our recent adventure, I'd agree. What did you think of him? Cruz?"

Lei splashed hot coffee on her hand and muttered a curse. "He was fine. Very helpful." She slurped the beverage, gathering her composure. Harry was sure to know something was up if she kept getting flustered at every mention of his name. Truth was, she had no romantic interest in Cruz, nor he in her from what she could tell. What they'd shared was simply a healing experience, if an extremely enjoyable one. She clung to that thought as she sorted through what to tell her new friend. "I actually had a bad situation going on with that blond guy I was dancing with. He was getting overly friendly, and Cruz helped me get rid of him. We took a walk on the beach after, and he showed me some moves to help me relax."

"I gotta say, Lei, you're a magnet for trouble." Harry eyed Lei over the rim of her coffee cup. "It's weird how that kind of perp seems to be drawn to you."

Lei sighed. "My therapist in San Rafael told me that research shows that, for some reason, women who are sexually abused as children often end up being victimized later, too."

"So that's what's wrong." Harry set her cup down. "I'm sorry that happened to you, Lei. That sucks." The baby began fussing, and Harry leaned over to pluck the infant out of the carrier with a movement that seemed entirely natural. She cuddled the tiny girl against her towel-clad body, cooing to her, then removed a full bottle from a thermal bag and fed the infant.

Lei watched in fascination. Harry seemed to be handling the child like a natural. "I'm done with all that stuff from my past. If this road trip showed me anything, it's that I want to be in control of my body. No one's going to mess with me ever again." She said it like a vow, each word a statement. "I wish I had more time to work with you and Cruz, learn more techniques. But I'm hoping my application to the police academy is accepted, and I can get those skills another way."

"Well, you look better, today. All bright-eyed and bushy-tailed." Harry rocked the baby gently as she fed her. "That's Cruz's specialty. He's all about being in the now and using your mind to control your reactions."

"I definitely need work on that. It feels good to have some things to try." Lei waved her coffee cup toward Harry and the baby. "What are you going to do about her?"

Harry gazed into the child's face. "I think I'll keep her."

Lei frowned. "Is that legal?"

Harry glanced up and her light brown eyes blazed. "Who's going to stop me?" With her chiseled shoulders, fierce gaze, and the looming, protective bulk of Kona at her side, she was intimidating.

"I'm sure there are procedures to adopt a baby," Lei mumbled. "Not that I have a clue what they'd be."

"Less is more sometimes," Harry said enigmatically. "I'm going to call her Malia. It means 'Still Waters' in Hawaiian, and she's a very calm baby."

"Yes, she is." Lei could only agree; Malia's mellow temperament made her easy to love, and clearly, Harry's heart had been lost to her.

The women finished their breakfast and Harry put the sleeping Malia back in her carrier and stood up. "Let me show you a simple *tai chi* routine you can use whenever you need to center yourself."

Harry was leading Lei through it, naming each of the moves and having her repeat it, when Kelly and Cruz returned to the pool area.

Lei had never seen Kelly so bedraggled. Her gym outfit was filthy, her ponytailed hair filled with sand and bits of grass, her face dripping sweat and red with exertion. Cruz, in contrast, looked cool and composed, only a tiny shine on his nose showing he'd been up to anything more than a stroll.

"Oh yes! Coffee!" Kelly exclaimed, pouncing on the carafe and splashing dark liquid into Lei's empty mug. "You two have been lounging over here while this dude was kicking my ass!"

"Just a few self-defense moves that I hope you never have to use," Cruz said. "After your recent situation, Harry and I wanted to be sure you two had a few more moves to help you get out of trouble."

Lei sneaked a glance at him as he picked up a grape from Harry's fruit bowl and tossed it into his mouth, showing a flash of those pearly teeth. He looked delicious, all chiseled muscles in a ninja-black outfit. He caught Lei's eye and smiled, and while there was mischief in his expression, there was also kindly regard. "You look well-rested, Lei."

"Yeah, I got a good night's sleep, thanks to you," Lei said, dimpling a little. "Your instruction was super helpful." She meant it sincerely.

"Happy to help. This was all we have time to do with you two, though. Harry and I need to get on the road."

Harry frowned. "I was hoping for another couple of days in the lap of luxury."

"Afraid not. We have a new job, and it's time to move on."

"Well, thanks, Cruz. Let me give you two something for your expenses. I'll run back and get my purse." Kelly trotted off, clearly invigorated by her lesson.

"We don't need her money. Got plenty of everything we need." Harry embraced Lei with the stiffness of someone who seldom touches others—Lei recognized it because she seldom did either.

"I'm so glad we met. I can't imagine what would have happened to us if you hadn't decided to help me go after those men," Lei told her.

"I hope our paths cross again someday," Harry said. "I'll just run to my room and pack. Would you keep an eye on Kona and Malia?"

Cruz seemed unsurprised about the development of a baby joining their little cadre, so Lei didn't think it was her place to comment. "Of course," Lei said. She turned back to Cruz as Harry sped off. "You're a talented teacher. I wish I had more time to train with you."

"It is not to be, but what was will remain," he said. "It's always a pleasure to have a student who's willing to take a chance and commit to something. You will be all right, now."

"Yes, I do believe I will." Lei stepped into his embrace as easily as if she'd never left it, and for a timeless moment, their hearts and breaths joined again in rhythm, as their foreheads rested against each other. Finally, their arms dropped and they stepped back. Lei gazed into Cruz's familiar, beautiful brown eyes, and felt his kindness.

"Be well," he said, with that little bow.

"You, too." Lei returned the gesture. Harry appeared, knapsack on her shoulder. She scooped up the baby carrier. Kona moved to her side. "I hope I see you again, Lei."

"Me too." Having a friend like Harry felt good. "How can I contact you?"

Harry smiled. "You can't. But our paths will cross again when the time is right."

Cruz, Harry and Kona moved off down the hotel's graveled walk to the beach and disappeared among the ornamental plantings.

Lei turned and headed back toward Kelly's bungalow, rubbing the smooth granite pebble between her fingers.

Yes, she would be fine. Maybe someday, thanks to Cruz, she'd even find love. But for now, she'd be happy with a dog, and hopefully Aunty would still want to get one.

CHAPTER TWELVE

Lᴇɪ ᴜɴʟᴏᴄᴋᴇᴅ the door and stepped inside Aunty Rosario's little house on D street in San Rafael. She unslung her duffle bag and lowered it to the floor, gazing down the short hallway with its overhead light on. She was tired from the long drive back from Mexico. Kelly had just dropped her at the curb, then continued on to her parents' house. "Aunty?"

Lei looked at the clock. After nine p.m. No, Aunty probably wasn't home from the restaurant yet.

She went down the hall and into her bedroom. The familiar sight of her little twin bed, her bureau with the row of bird nests on it, her desk under the window . . . all of it gave her a feeling of comfort.

It was almost as if the tumultuous events of the last ten days had been some kind of dream—more like a nightmare, except for a few key scenes, starring an enigmatic man named Cruz. Lei couldn't help smiling at the memory of her experience with him on the Cabo San Lucas beach.

She unzipped her duffle and pulled out the clothing stuffed inside, sorting all the dirty clothes into a pile on the floor, and the tightly rolled, clean ones to be returned to the bureau. She took out the heavy combat blade she had taken from Joao, and her Glock, secure in its plastic case.

She needed to get training with these weapons pronto; if only she could have had more time with Harry and Cruz! Where were they going next, with Kona and baby Malia? Would she ever see them again?

A key rattled in the lock, and the front door opened. "Lei? Is that you?" There was an unfamiliar note in her aunt's voice: *apprehension*. Could it even be fear?

"It's me, Aunty!" Lei called. "Come back to my room and get your souvenir present!"

Rosario's steps hurried down the hall. A moment later, Lei was embracing her beloved aunt's sturdy form, pressing her cheek onto her aunt's curly head.

"I'm so glad you're back," Aunty said, muffled against Lei's shoulder, her body vibrating with tension.

Lei had not apprised Rosario of any part of the crazy adventure she and Kelly had been on down in Mexico. She had sent two postcards from the resort, which probably hadn't even reached Aunty yet, so there was no way Rosario had a clue what Lei had been through. What was worrying her aunt? Lei stepped back, holding Rosario's shoulders. "What's wrong?"

Rosario shook her head, smiling in a forced way. "Nothing I want to bother you with right now. Show me this present."

Lei turned around and lifted a hat off the bed, setting it right on top of Aunty's head. Her gift to Rosario was a well-made Panama cowboy hat, decorated with a leather band set with silver conchos inlaid with turquoise. "A little something to honor your *paniolo* heritage, Aunty."

Aunty Rosario and Lei's father, Wayne Texeira, had grown up on the Big Island of Hawaii. Their parents had been a Hawaiian woman and a Portuguese cowboy who came to work on the big Waimea cattle ranches. The siblings had grown up in that lifestyle, and Aunty still talked about their riding and roping days on their employers' ranch.

Aunty quickly removed the hat from her head to admire it. "Oh, Lei, I couldn't love it more! This is such a beautiful hat, where did you find it?"

"It wasn't easy." Lei flopped down on the bed, and described the day at the markets that she and Kelly had spent, combing through various cheap souvenir stands for one that carried authentic cowboy hats with Mexican worked silver to enhance them. Lei was happy to be able to tell Rosario a real story about what had happened down there, since she had no intention of burdening her aunt with the murder and mayhem they'd survived.

"I love it." Aunty clasped the hat to her chest. Lei met her gaze, and Rosario's eyes were still worried. "I have to go around and make sure everything is locked up."

Lei frowned. "Have there been more break-ins?"

"Yes. Whoever is raiding our neighborhood is even bolder, now." Aunty sighed. "I didn't want to tell you right away, but it's so on my mind, and I want you to be prepared in case we need to defend ourselves."

"What happened?"

"Our neighbor's place was broken into while they were asleep in their beds! They were tied up while the thieves went through their house. The police are investigating, and they've put extra patrol cars in our neighborhood, but I'm afraid that our house could be next."

Lei had counted on feeling safe when she got home! She reached into her pocket to rub the stone Cruz had given her. "What about that plan you were thinking about to get a dog?"

Rosario met Lei's eyes. "I know you wanted for us to take time to think about it, but I actually have a dog arranged to come visit us on a trial basis. She will be delivered by the adoption service tomorrow."

"She?"

"Yes. She is an eighteen-month-old Rottweiler. She washed out of police training because her nose is not sharp enough to pick up the scents of different kinds of substances. They wanted to use her for various kinds of location and tracking, as well as a police dog, but her sense of smell just isn't strong enough, though in every other way, she qualified for their program."

"A dog. Tomorrow!" Lei's heart thumped with excitement. "I made a new friend on the trip—another Hawaii girl. Her name was Harry, and she had a dog named Kona." It was safe to share that much; so she told her aunt about Kona and how much she'd liked him. "After getting to know Kona a little bit and seeing how fun it could be to have a dog, I'd changed my mind, Aunty, and I was going to propose that we adopt one for sure. If I qualify for the police job on the Big Island, either you can keep her with you, or I will take her with me. Thanks so much for doing all the paperwork and getting through the hoops. I'm sure there were a lot of them, to adopt a trained animal like that."

"It wasn't just an adoption process," Aunty said, "there was a lottery. But I was lucky enough to win her on a trial basis."

"What should we name her?" Lei asked.

"I think it's a little premature for that," Aunty said. "They warned me that she's going to be a lot of dog to handle. They're going to have to train us, too, on how to work with her. But I'm feeling hopeful about it. At the very least, I know I'll sleep better at night with a big Rottweiler in the house to bark at anybody trying to get in."

"You and me both," Lei said.

They spent a restless night that night, sharing Aunty's bed for the first time since the first year when Lei had come to her aunt's as a traumatized child. Even so, Lei woke up at every scratch of a branch at the window. She couldn't wait to meet their new dog and have an animal's sharp eyes and ears watching out for them.

CHAPTER THIRTEEN

LEI AND AUNTY were waiting on the front porch of Aunty's bungalow when a van with 'K-9 Training Center' on the side of it pulled up in front of their house the next morning.

A young man dressed in a blue uniform with the same logo as the van on his pocket stepped out to greet them. His name, he told them, was Josh. "And meet Kali."

Josh opened the sliding door, and they got their first glimpse of the dog that would be spending the next week with them.

Lei had not been prepared for how beautiful a young Rottweiler in the prime of its life could be. Kali had the classic markings of the breed: a sleek black coat, a bobbed tail, feet and chest in a rich chestnut that matched her eyebrow patches. The Rottie sat quietly, gazing at them with large, intelligent brown eyes. Her solid body gleamed from head to toe with good health and solid musculature. Her folded ears were pricked, her nose shiny. Small brown patches above her eyes accented an expression of interest and intelligence.

The trainer clipped a leash onto Kali's chain collar, and she hopped down from the van to step to his side. He introduced them, and Lei held a closed fist down for the dog to sniff.

"We have been calling her Kali," Josh said. "So if you do keep her, and you don't like that name, whatever you name her should have a similar hard 'K' sound and an 'i' at the end."

Lei instinctively didn't like the name; though it was a good one for such a guard dog as this, that of a fierce goddess of death, it didn't suit the gentle feeling Lei got from the dog. This sweet girl was going to be named something uniquely Hawaii, uniquely theirs. "Show us what she can do."

The trainer demonstrated how Kali could patrol the house or yard at a hand signal, go into defense mode to guard their house with another command, come, sit, stay, and aggressively "hold" an intruder by backing them into a corner and keeping them there.

"Kali failed our standards for tracking," he said regretfully. "It's too bad, because she's a bright dog with a great disposition. She will work for you until she drops once you have her loyalty. But you must dominate her regularly; be her leader. Rotties can become bullies if they're unsure who's the boss. Here's how you will do that."

He showed them how to establish a leadership role with Kali using commands and treats. "You should practice her training with her often."

Lei felt comfortable with this new way of relating to an animal, while Aunty struggled. "If she tries to herd me, I think I'll just want to go where she wants me to go," Aunty said, laughing.

"Rottweilers are very strong-willed and need a firm, loving hand, and clear leadership," Josh told them. "If you let her push you around, she will become the alpha, and then . . . all the training we've put into her could be lost."

"I have no problem with that." Lei gave the hand signal for the dog to come, and then she had Kali lay down at her side. Lei went through the different hand and voice signals again, and then finally gave Kali a treat, as the trainer encouraged her to do. "I'll go through these exercises with her every day."

"Good! That is just what we want to hear. She's young, so to be her best she also needs a lot of exercise—a vigorous walk for an hour or so, at least once a day."

"I'm a runner. I'll take her jogging with me." Lei was thrilled at the idea of moving down the road with the dog at her side.

Josh went to the van and removed a small bag containing some toys, a spare leash, and a sample bag of the food Kali had been eating. "I will be checking in with you at the end of the week to see if you want to keep her. Don't worry if she's not a fit; there is a list a mile long of people who want to adopt her. So, make sure you can handle a dog that needs this level of active commitment."

Lei was already sure that she wanted the beautiful Rottweiler more than she had wanted anything for a very long time. "We'll be in touch."

The van drove off, and Lei and Aunty looked down at their new dog. "First things first. You're getting a new name, as of today, and I know just the thing. I'm going to call you Keiki," Lei said. "Child, in Hawaiian. Because you're our Keiki girl."

Aunty knelt beside the Rottie and stroked her ears. Keiki leaned against her, and Rosario smiled up at Lei. "Keiki is perfect, and we both know she's your dog, not mine. She can be your girl, until you have your own child someday."

Lei rolled her eyes. "That'll be the day."

"Life has a way of surprising us," Rosario said. "Just wait and see."

CHAPTER FOURTEEN

L‌EI PROMPTLY PUT Keiki on the leash and took the Rottweiler out for a run.

The experience was very different from running alone; Lei was used to a feeling of invisibility as she jogged down the road, her earbuds in place, her expression blank as she hid beneath the brim of a ballcap.

But with Keiki at her side, people noticed her. They looked at the beautiful dog, and some of them moved away to give the two of them a wide berth, apprehensive about a large, muscular animal with a reputation for being a guard dog. Others were dog lovers, and smiled at the sight of the two of them. All in all, Lei enjoyed the feeling of companionship she felt moving through the world with Keiki at her side.

Keiki stayed level with Lei, only occasionally trying to step ahead in a way that Josh had cautioned was a bid for leadership. Lei checked the Rottie with the chain collar, and Keiki fell back to trot at her side, reassured by Lei's position as the alpha in their little duo.

When they came to a stoplight, and Lei jogged in place, Keiki stood quietly or sat on her haunches, waiting for the light to change.

Traffic signals were clearly not something new to her; she seemed to recognize the changing of the lights and had an appreciation for cars, as well as for other people on the sidewalk. Occasionally, Keiki would glance up at Lei, a slight scrunch on her broad brow, as if asking if everything was all right.

"It sure is, girl," Lei said. "I'm so glad to have you with me."

Lei had never felt as safe and comfortable out in the world as she did with Keiki by her side. The connection she'd felt as soon as their eyes met only got stronger.

Back at the house, Aunty Rosario and Lei established a bed for Keiki in the living room, a good spot for the Rottweiler to keep an eye on the premises.

"Do you think we should also put in an alarm system?" Aunty asked. The worry lines between her brows had relaxed a bit since Keiki arrived, but they weren't yet gone.

"It's up to you, Aunty. There will be times when I have her away from the house, and if you want it to be watched, we can always do that."

"Let's wait and see how she does. When we're both at the restaurant working, or you have your classes, Keiki will be here alone, guarding the house."

"I think I would much rather face an alarm system if I were a burglar than Keiki."

Aunty nodded. "Me too."

Lei ran Keiki through her commands twice a day, and three days went by as they settled into a nice rhythm. When they left Keiki in the house alone, she barked when they first came home, a scary sound, but quickly quieted when she recognized their voices or footsteps. Her whole body wagged in greeting when they opened the door, and sometimes she whimpered with happiness.

That was a wonderful feeling that Lei hadn't expected; Keiki's joy in the simplest things made Lei happy, too.

What if the adoption service wanted to take Keiki back for some reason? Lei couldn't handle the stress of that idea, so on the morning of their fourth day together, she called up the trainer.

"We absolutely love her," she told Josh. "Whatever we need to sign, send it over. I can't stand the thought of anyone taking her away."

Josh laughed. "I thought I saw that spark between the two of you when you met," he said. "I'm happy to hear it. Your aunt has completed all the necessary paperwork. We will just check Kali off as a successful adoption. I will still leave it open for the ten days, in case you change your mind."

"I'm not going to change my mind," Lei said. "And her new name is Keiki."

LEI'S CLASSES were about to resume, and other than a few texts, she hadn't heard from Kelly. How was her friend doing after their ordeal in Mexico? Kelly would make light of it if Lei asked her directly— she had to see her friend to really know.

Lei called Kelly. "I have a surprise," she told her friend. "Meet me at the county park near the bridge."

"What is this? Please tell me you're dating someone."

Lei laughed. "You could say that. But it won't be what you're thinking."

"This I gotta see. Meet you in an hour."

Lei and Keiki jogged down to the county park—a small, tidy expanse tucked inside a redwood grove beside the stores and restaurants of old town San Rafael. Spreading maple trees over the sidewalk were just beginning to fully leaf in with the changing of spring into summer, and the flower beds were filled in with bright blossoms as they arrived at the little park.

Kelly jogged up to meet them and clapped her hands to her cheeks in surprise. "Omigosh, Lei, what a beautiful dog!"

Keiki sat when Lei gave her a hand signal, but her tongue hung out in a big happy grin as she gazed at Kelly. Lei was becoming attuned to the way Keiki communicated with her expressive face and clear body language. "She likes you," Lei told Kelly. "You can pet her if you want."

"I'm not sure. I'm a little scared of dogs, and she is so big."

"Keiki's a sweetheart. She can be a fierce guardian, though we haven't seen that side of her yet. We're really glad to have her since those break-ins started in our neighborhood."

Kelly approached as Lei directed, with her hand down and in a fist held out for Keiki to sniff. The dog gave her fingers a lick, and Kelly giggled; but as Lei peered at her friend, she spotted dark circles ringing Kelly's eyes, and her friend had lost weight.

"Let's sit on the bench," Lei said.

Kelly sat beside Keiki and petted her chest and ears. Keiki leaned on her legs the way she did when she liked someone.

Lei frowned. "You don't look like you've been sleeping well."

"I haven't been." Kelly shook her head. "It's like everything that happened to us in Mexico has caught up with me. I thought I was fine when we were at the resort . . . but I'm having all sorts of bad dreams and flashbacks. I was even paranoid jogging down here to the park." She patted her pocket. "I have a big pepper spray in there, and a shock device in my other pocket."

"I'm not saying it's not a good idea to have a few weapons on you, especially after what we've been through. But I hope you're getting some professional help, too." Lei had considered it herself but running and channeling her memories into the little rock that she always carried in her pocket had seemed to be enough for now.

"I contacted the college. They have a sexual abuse survivor group. I'm going to that. It's been really helpful to hear other people's stories. You should come, Lei."

Lei felt a prickling of alarm on the back of her neck. "I don't know. I'm not a group kind of person. I'll think about it."

She had so much more than the one incident in Mexico banging around in the back of her brain. She might remember more about what Charlie Kwon had done to her, and she didn't want to. If she opened that door, it could all come tumbling out and take over her life, and she was not about to let that happen. *He'd stolen enough from her.*

Kelly stood up. "They say it helps to tell your story, but I don't want to tell our story in the group . . . because you know—murder and everything."

"You and I didn't kill anyone," Lei said softly. "Harry did. Harry also took the baby, which I'm pretty sure was illegal. I'm not saying that was a bad thing, and I don't know what else she could have done that would have been better for the baby. I've heard the orphanages are bad down there. Harry obviously fell in love with the baby, and I'm sure she'll give the kid a good home. But the whole thing . . . it's just not something we should ever talk about."

"I was thinking the same thing," Kelly said. "In the group I just talked about the actual attack on the two of us, and how they kidnapped me, and what they did to me. The first time I told what happened, it felt good, like I had this giant . . . I don't know what, like a boil or something—it popped, and all this poison came out."

"Now that's just gross," Lei said, and they both laughed.

It felt good to laugh.

"I told my parents that I was stressed out, and I wanted to go to personal therapy, too. I researched a method for traumatic memories called EMDR," Kelly said. "It's new. It's cutting-edge. Maybe it will help."

"That's great. Let me know how it goes." But once again, Lei felt that prickling. She wasn't ready to deal with her past, with all that had happened to her eleven years ago, let alone with what had happened to her in Mexico just two weeks ago.

The girls jogged all the way back to Kelly's house with Keiki at their side. Kelly patted the dog's head as they said goodbye. "I sure feel safe and secure with her," Kelly said. "Did you see how people go way around us?"

"It makes me a little sad," Lei said. "Keiki is so well-trained. She would never attack someone unless I told her to."

"Well maybe you're the one people need to be afraid of," Kelly said, and they both laughed again.

CHAPTER FIFTEEN

Lᴇɪ ᴀɴsᴡᴇʀᴇᴅ the door in the afternoon of the following day. An older couple stood on the porch, holding a clipboard. Both plump, gray-haired, and dressed in California casual, they had identical anxious expressions on their pale faces. "Hi. Is Rosario at home?" the woman asked.

"I'm sorry, no. She's at the restaurant. Can I help?"

Behind her, Keiki crowded close, her chest rumbling with an incipient growl at the sight of possible intruders. Lei lowered a hand to her side and snapped her fingers. Keiki settled onto her haunches, waiting for a signal.

"Oh, that's too bad. She knew about our project, organizing a neighborhood patrol against those robbers that have come into our area," the older woman said. "My name is Liza, and this is my husband, Gregory."

"I'm Lei, Rosario's niece, and this is our dog, Keiki." Lei gestured for Keiki to come forward to meet the couple. Both of them stepped backward nervously, and Lei held up a hand. "Keiki is a very well-trained guard dog. We got her after the burglaries began. She would never hurt you."

The two were eventually persuaded to step forward and let Keiki sniff them. Gregory tentatively patted Keiki's shiny head, giving her a scratch behind her ears.

"Well, since Rosario isn't here, can we tell you what we're organizing? Maybe you and Keiki can help us with our project," Liza said.

"Sure. Let's all get comfortable." Lei gestured them to a set of wicker furniture, a little dusty and covered with leaves, out on the porch. She brushed off the cushions, and the three sat, Keiki beside Lei in her armchair.

Gregory leaned forward, resting his elbows on his knees, and cleared his throat. "Perhaps Rosario told you about our home invasion. The robbers broke into our house while we were sleeping. When we woke up, they forced us out of bed, and tied us up. They put us in the closet. I wasn't able to tell the police much about them, except that it was two male perpetrators—they were wearing ski masks. They were also armed."

"That is so scary and very serious," Lei said. "I'm so glad you weren't injured! Yes, Aunty did tell me about that. We've both slept better since we got Keiki to keep an eye on our house."

All of them looked at the beautiful Rottweiler, sitting upright beside Lei with a curious expression in her brown eyes, her head tilted as if she understood every word they were saying.

"Anyway, the police know all about it, and it's an open case—but we're not convinced the burglars are done with our area," Gregory said.

"I'm not convinced of that either," Lei said.

"Our therapist suggested that we take some action steps so that we don't just feel like we've been . . . victimized, for lack of a better word," Liza said. "So that inspired us to take this on."

"Is that what this project is about?"

"Yes." Liza held up the clipboard. "We are organizing nighttime foot patrols of the neighborhood. We're asking our friends and neighbors to go in pairs throughout the area of the burglaries. We have gotten approval and support from the police for this plan, and we have a direct line to the patrol cars assigned to our neighborhood. When someone who is walking this neighborhood sees something suspicious, they are to contact the patrol cars assigned to us right away."

Lei's pulse picked up. Supporting the neighborhood patrol seemed perfect, now that she had Keiki to walk with. "Keiki and I can take a shift, for sure. How big is the area?"

Gregory took a map out from underneath the forms on top of the clipboard and showed Lei the streets they would be patrolling. "The police strongly suggested that we work in pairs."

Lei reached down to pet Keiki's broad chest. "Keiki and I make a pair."

"You two *are* the perfect pair." The older man smiled for the first time. Lei could see what a pleasant face he had when the stress around his eyes had disappeared; his wrinkles were those earned by good living and humor. The robbers had stolen a lot more than belongings from this couple.

Lei told them that Aunty Rosario would not be available for the neighborhood patrol because of her nighttime work at the restaurant, and her age. "My Aunty needs all the rest she can get when she's home from work," Lei explained.

"We understand. We would be snug in our beds too if we weren't so worried about what could happen. We won't sleep well until those perps are behind bars," Liza said. "Having you and Keiki is the best signup we've had yet."

Lei filled out the forms, and signed a waiver agreeing to call the police immediately and not engage with any criminals herself. "That's very important," Greg cautioned. "No matter how tempted you are to confront the robbers, the police told us not to. They were armed when they took us prisoner, in our own home. We don't want any of our neighborhood patrol people getting hurt in this endeavor."

"I understand," Lei said. The couple said goodbye, smiling and waving, and left a map of the streets Lei and Keiki would begin patrolling from eight till midnight. Lei showed Keiki the map. "We better get a nap this afternoon, girl. We are going to need it for the graveyard shift."

LIZA AND GREG had told Lei that the patrollers should be easily visible by wearing reflective clothing and carrying a lit flashlight. Part of what the neighborhood patrol was doing was prevention through warding off intruders, discouraging them from coming into the area at all.

But Lei had a different plan: she wanted to catch these guys in the act.

At eight p.m., she dressed carefully all in black: a turtleneck, hiking pants, and athletic shoes so that she could run efficiently, as well as a billed black cap that hid her face. She and Keiki set off at a slow jog.

Lei held a flashlight but kept it off; Greg and Liza had told her to keep the flashlight swinging back and forth but Lei did not obey these instructions. She carried pepper spray in her pocket and in a shoulder holster, her Glock, which she was licensed to carry concealed. The big Buck knife from Mexico was strapped around her ankle.

If she was lucky enough to confront the robbers, Lei was armed and dangerous.

Well. At least, Keiki was dangerous.

Beside Lei, Keiki trotted quietly in work mode, her eyes forward, her ears pricked, her nose sniffing, her body alert.

They moved steadily down quiet streets lined with the nineteen twenties bungalows built when San Rafael had been a sleepy suburb of San Francisco, not yet the bustling, busy town it had grown into. Old-growth oak and maple trees shielded the road, casting pools of darkness as the pair crunched across a few leaves. A night breeze lifted the brim of Lei's hat and fluttered Keiki's ears; an occasional car swished by.

All was quiet.

Their four hours of patrol passed relatively quickly. Lei waved to the brightly lit up, well-dressed couple in reflective clothing who replaced her on the patrol, and she and Keiki reentered Aunty's house.

Lei had trouble unwinding afterward. She got online and researched the robberies, reading old police blotter reports and studying the pattern that the burglars had been following. There was a geographical element to it; the break-ins had begun to the south, and the burglars had been working steadily towards this area. They took jewelry, small antiques, cash, and portable electronics. "They must be fencing this stuff somewhere," Lei muttered. "I wonder what the police are doing?" She couldn't wait to have her own cases and dig into her own leads and ideas someday. "Find the outlet for these stolen items, and that could lead to the source of them."

Maybe the police were investigating like Lei would have if it was her case; maybe all they needed to do was wait. Lei fell asleep at last, in front of her monitor, her head propped on her arms.

CHAPTER SIXTEEN

CLASSES HAD RESUMED for Lei's college program, and she muddled through the next day without enough sleep. Now, she and Keiki were on patrol again, and this time, she didn't have the energy for jogging.

She and Keiki walked the quiet neighborhood, lit by pools of streetlight, and Lei sipped from a thermos mug of coffee. Her mind was occupied with the letter she had received that afternoon: the police academy on the Big Island had accepted her application.

Lei was excited, which created a little churn in her stomach, helping to counteract tiredness. She was also worried; not only was the date for her departure only two weeks away, but she would have to leave in the middle of the semester, not yet completing her criminal justice degree and taking incompletes on her classes. Worst of all, she would be leaving Aunty Rosario to face this threat from the robbers by herself, without Keiki for protection if she shipped the dog over with her. They would have to navigate the quarantine program for moving dogs to Hawaii. Maybe what she should do was go over by herself and bring Keiki to the Big Island after the robbers had been caught. "If they get caught," she muttered. Keiki looked up at her questioningly, and Lei patted her head. "Never mind, girl. I'm sure we'll catch them soon."

Lei had been too stressed out by receiving the letter to talk to Aunty about the situation; it helped that Rosario was still at the restaurant when they'd left on patrol.

Lei was distracted, so she almost missed seeing a dart of movement out of the corner of her eye—but Keiki stopped abruptly, a growl rumbling in her broad chest.

Lei tweaked her leash and they fell back into a black pool of darkness cast by one of the sheltering oak trees that shaded the sidewalk during the day.

There it was again . . . a tiny flash of light, as if from a penlight, at the side of one of the bungalows only three houses down from Aunty's place.

Lei was suddenly wide awake.

She pressed against the rough bark of the tree, quieting Keiki as they focused on the activity near the house's window.

This was their chance to catch the robbers! Determined as Lei was to confront the robbers herself, they needed backup. She fumbled her phone out of her pocket, calling the direct line they had to the police patrols in their area.

Lei whispered the location and address to the dispatcher, and told them that she saw an attempted break-in happening. She asked for the police to come quickly and keep their lights and sirens off. The dispatcher told Lei a unit would be there shortly; she should stay back and observe.

"Of course," Lei said—but she had no intention of doing that.

Sliding her phone into her pocket, Lei and Keiki headed stealthily toward the disturbance. Lei slid her flashlight—the large, heavy metal type used by police officers as a weapon as well as a light source—out of its belt loop. She raised the light to shoulder level, readying to flash it on the burglars.

She and Keiki moved closer, sliding quietly across the soft grass of the bungalow's lawn. Lei rested a restraining hand on Keiki's head as the dog persisted in a low growl; she didn't want the perps to hear them as they sneaked to the side of the house near the activity.

In the dim moonlight, two dark figures were setting a ladder against the side of the house. Lei waited until one of the figures was on the ladder before she moved in as closely as she dared, hitting the flashlight's ON button.

The blinding beam illuminated two men dressed all in black and wearing ski masks. The brightness that froze the two men also burned Lei's retinas. "Stop right where you are! Police are on their way!" Lei yelled at full volume. Keiki lunged forward, snarling and barking, a ferocious and terrifying sound.

The robber on the ladder lost his grip and fell to the ground with a cry. The one steadying the ladder spun around to face them—and he held a weapon in his hand.

Keiki strained at the end of the leash, eager to sink her teeth into someone. *But if Lei let her go, the robber would shoot her dog!* Lei couldn't let go of Keiki's leash. Her only chance was to intimidate the men into surrender.

"Drop your weapon!" Lei shouted. "Drop it now!"

The robber fired the gun.

The loudness of the pistol's report stole Lei's breath. She threw herself down over Keiki instinctively, bearing the startled dog to the ground. She ran her hands over the squirming Rottweiler, terrified that the dog had been shot—but Keiki struggled to get to her feet and pursue her quarry. "Down, girl!"

Lei had her hands full, keeping control of Keiki and still terrified of her dog being shot. The robber who'd fallen scrambled to his feet with the help of the one holding the gun, and the two men ran for it, their legs illuminated for a moment in the fallen flashlight's beam.

House lights came on inside the bungalow, and a screech of tires at the sidewalk alerted Lei to the arrival of the police.

Lei sat up, pulling Keiki in close, rubbing her dog's chest and calming her. Keiki vibrated with rage and passion to catch the robbers, still growling. Her dog had never even flinched at the terrible sound of the gunshot, but Lei trembled with shock at how close they might've come to being killed.

Two officers stormed up onto the lawn. "Identify yourself!"

Lei stood up, still holding Keiki's leash, but raising her empty free hand. "I'm with the neighborhood watch! I'm the one that called you. The robbers are running, and they went that way!" The officers took off in the direction Lei pointed.

Lei ran her hands down Keiki's sides, checking her all over for injury—her dog was sweating and trembling, her muscular body vibrating. "It's okay, girl. You did good. Settle down, now."

That had been close—too close.

The owners of the house ran out onto their porch in their pajamas: a couple and a teenage boy, all of them holding baseball bats.

Lei hesitantly approached, Keiki tight against her side. "Your house was about to be invaded," Lei said. "The robbers were getting in up that ladder to the window. I'm with the neighborhood watch. I was able to call the police in time."

"What was that gunshot?" the father of the house exclaimed.

"They took a shot at us." Lei's whole body burst out in sweat and she began to tremble. "I shined my light on them, and they ran away."

"I'm on the neighborhood patrol, too," the man said, coming down from the porch. "Are you injured? Did they hit you or your dog?"

"Thanks, we're okay."

The man took in her all-black outfit. "Aren't you supposed to be wearing reflective clothing?"

"I missed the memo on that," Lei lied.

Soon the police officers came trotting back. "They got away."

Lei submitted a statement, and was subjected to a lecture and an interview about everything she had seen and done. She and Keiki were thoroughly chastened when they finally walked back to Aunty's house.

Lei took a long, hot shower. She then wiped Keiki down with disinfectant pet wipes to cool her and get the sweat off her fur. Lei let

Keiki up on her bed for the first time—needing the closeness of the dog beside her, needing to have her hand on Keiki's back, feeling the Rottweiler's heartbeat, knowing that she was safe and alive.

Lei had needlessly endangered herself and her beloved animal. Tomorrow night would be very different.

CHAPTER SEVENTEEN

LEI DRAGGED herself out into the kitchen the next morning, relieved to see that Aunty was up and had made a big pot of coffee. "Did you hear about all the excitement last night, Aunty?"

Aunty yawned. "No, I was at the restaurant until ten p.m., so by the time I got home, you and Keiki were in bed. What happened?"

Lei poured herself a cup of coffee, pondering how much to share. "Keiki and I caught the robbers in the act. We called the police on them, and they almost got busted. At least we prevented another break-in at a house three down from us."

"What!" Aunty almost dropped her cup into the sink. "I hope you two are okay?"

"Well, as I told you, we're only supposed to call the police," Lei hedged. She felt that blush that always gave her away burning her cheeks and ears, so she avoided looking at Aunty. "They were armed with at least one gun. I'm sure you would have woken up at the sound of the gunshot if you were home, because they shot at us."

Aunty hurried to hug Lei, squeezing her close. "Oh honey!"

Lei couldn't lie to her aunt. "Aunty, it was my fault. I wasn't supposed to, but I wanted to be the one to bust those men. So, I caught them in my flashlight beam and told them to stop what they

99

were doing. It almost seemed like it was working, until . . . one of the guys fired at us."

Aunty swayed on her feet, going pale. Lei held her up. "Aunty! Are you okay? I'm so sorry. I did such a stupid thing. I promise I won't take chances like that tonight when we're on patrol!"

"You can't go! I won't let you!"

"But Aunty, I'm going to become a police officer. This is all practice for that, and . . . while I'm telling you things—I got the acceptance letter from the Hawaii Police Academy. I start in two weeks."

Rosario reached for one of the kitchen chairs and fell into it like a bag of laundry. "I need some more coffee."

Lei hurried over and filled Aunty's cup with fresh brew, then came and sat down next to her. Keiki, sensing that the women were upset, padded over to lean against Aunty Rosario's legs, laying her head in Rosario's lap and looking up with soulful eyes. Aunty's hand stroked the Rottweiler's broad forehead, her fingers playing with Keiki's silky ears. "What am I going to do without the two of you?"

"I've been thinking, Aunty. I don't feel good about taking Keiki away while we still have this threat. So I'll fly over to Hawaii by myself so that I can figure things out, like a place to live. Keiki has to go through a quarantine process for our move anyway, so she can stay here with you for a while. I will find myself an apartment and get started with the training, and when we know that these robbers have been captured, that's when Keiki can come over and join me."

Aunty glanced at Lei. Her brown eyes, ones that Lei saw in the mirror every day on her own face, were deeply sad. "I don't want you to go, Lei-girl. Are you sure you can't just join the California police department?"

Lei set her hand over Aunty's, resting on top of Keiki's head. "I need to go to Hilo, where it all began. I have to go, Aunty, to figure out . . . myself, things about my past. I have a feeling that will help me move forward in life."

Aunty heaved a gusty sigh. "I understand, but I don't have to like it." She reached over and grabbed a tissue from a nearby box on the table, and blew her nose.

Lei found herself blowing her nose too. "I wish you would come with me."

Aunty rolled her eyes. "After all I've been through building this restaurant and establishing myself here in San Rafael? No. This is my home now, though a part of my heart will always live in the *paniolo* country of Waimea."

Lei leaned over to kiss Aunty's forehead. "At least you'll have Keiki to keep you company and protect you while I'm gone."

"For a while, at least." Aunty blew her nose again. "Good thing I have lots of friends at the restaurant."

CHAPTER EIGHTEEN

TWO WEEKS LATER . . .

Lei staggered comically under the towering stack of leis draped around her neck as she looped an arm around her aunt.

"Haven't been lei'd this much since I graduated high school," she laughed, pushing the mountain of flower lei, paper lei, yarn lei, origami lei, crochet lei, candy lei and feather boas down enough to grin over the pile as she posed for a picture beside Aunty Rosario.

Rosario, wearing her trademark plumeria print apron and a chef's hat in matching fabric, wiped tears off her cheeks without shame. "So proud of my girl!"

"You'd think I graduated from the Hawaii Police Academy, but I'm just leaving for it," Lei said, with an expansive gesture. "Thanks so much for coming and making this night so special."

The packed restaurant, closed for business except to friends and family for Lei's going-away party, erupted in cheers and congratulations. Lei's aunty's extensive *'ohana* of friends and mainland relatives loved nothing more than an excuse to gather for food and fellowship.

A *pule* (prayer) by Aunty opened the buffet, and soon the

crowded room sorted itself into a boisterous line, with Lei and Aunty at the head.

"I want to see your plate filled with your favorite beef and pineapple stew," Momi, Aunty's restaurant partner, said. She handed Lei one of the deep china bowls. "And lots of rice to soak it up. Made 'em special for you, girl."

"Thank you, Aunty Momi," Lei leaned forward to kiss the Hawaiian woman's cheek. "Your stew is my favorite."

"And you always say *my* stew is your favorite!" Rosario protested, giving Lei a little shove.

"I get to have two favorites, don't I?" Lei laughed. "I'm going to miss you both, and this place, so much."

"Don't think about it until you have to," Momi advised. "And never forget, we're always here whenever you want to come home."

Later, seated beside Aunty at one of the crowded tables listening to one of her distant cousins from Las Vegas play slack-key guitar, Lei glanced at the clock over the door.

Eight p.m. Still early.

Keiki was home, locked inside the house, but this time of night they were usually patrolling the neighborhood. The robbers had gone quiet in the last two weeks, with no new incidents since they'd almost been captured by the police—but Lei was worried about leaving the dog home alone without her.

A weird sense of urgency drove her to her feet. "Aunty, I'm going to excuse myself and jog home super quick. Just to check on Keiki," she whispered in Rosario's ear. "I'll be back before you know it."

"All right." Rosario patted Lei's shoulder absently, her attention on the talented musician weaving a spell from the restaurant's little stage as he launched into a rendition of "Going to a Hukilau." Another cousin got up, encouraged by the family, to dance hula to the song.

Feeling guilty for leaving even for a few minutes, Lei slipped into the kitchen, unloaded the pile of leis onto the polished metal counter, grabbed her jacket, and exited out the back door.

LEI APPROACHED the little brown bungalow with its attached garage. Aunty had driven them to the restaurant tonight and had closed the garage door behind them. The overhead security light was on, as usual. Lei stepped up onto the little porch and inserted her key into the metal screen security door they'd installed over the regular front door once the break-ins had started—and that's when she heard Keiki inside, snarling and growling.

Lei froze, her eyes widening, her key inserted.

Something was very wrong.

CHAPTER NINETEEN

LEI PAUSED, one hand against the metal grill of the door, the other clenched around the key inserted into the lock. Inside the house, Keiki was still snarling and growling . . . but not barking.

Was Keiki afraid? Was there another animal inside, like a raccoon?

Lei turned the key, shouting, "Keiki!"

At the sound of her voice, the dog burst into loud, rapid barking. Lei recognized the same bark Keiki had used when confronting the robbers: *someone was in the house!*

Lei fumbled her flip phone out of her pocket, thankful that she had slipped it in there when she left the restaurant. Her fingers seemed unable to find the buttons as she fumbled to call the police. She brought the phone to her ear as she opened the grilled security door, then inserted her key into the lock on the wooden front door.

"Nine-one-one Emergency."

"There's someone inside our house! My dog is confronting them. Please hurry!" Lei gave the address.

"Do not enter the house," the operator directed. "Stay outside, if you suspect there is an intruder and your dog has engaged with them."

"But the robbers in our neighborhood have been armed!" Lei cried. "I don't want them to hurt my dog."

"A patrol is on their way to your location," the operator said. "Stay outside!"

Lei flipped her phone shut and slid it into her pocket.

She would do no such thing; she had to make sure that Keiki was safe.

Her hands were sweaty on the doorknob and Keiki's ferocious sounds made Lei even more nervous. She fumbled the door open. Peeking around it into the dimly lit front room, she called out, "Keiki?"

The Rottweiler renewed her barking, clearly trying to communicate something to Lei. The sounds were coming from the back of the bungalow. Had the robbers trapped Keiki in one of the bedrooms? Could they, even now, be roaming around inside the house?

Lei's heart thundered and she patted her pockets, frustrated that she had left her pepper spray and her weapon stashed safely in the glove box of the car. She was unarmed.

Lei scanned around the front room, spotting a big brass poker next to the rarely used fireplace. She darted over and picked it up, swinging the metal rod to her shoulder, baseball style.

Her athletic shoes squeaked on the linoleum of the kitchen as she walked on tiptoe into the hallway on the other side.

Keiki was definitely in one of the bedrooms or the bathroom, judging by her loud barking. The bedrooms off the hall were closed, as usual, but Aunty's room door was ajar, and the barking seemed to be coming from inside. Aunty had her own bathroom attached to the back of the room; could Keiki be trapped there?

Lei crept toward Aunty's bedroom. The dog's voice sounded too loud to be muffled by a door. She scanned everywhere as she crept down the hall but saw no sign of movement.

Perhaps the robbers had trapped Keiki inside, and left.

Lei's heart pounding was almost as loud as the sound of the

Rottweiler barking as she tiptoed forward, gently pushing Aunty's bedroom door wide.

On the other side of Aunty's bed, dressed in an antique Hawaiian pineapple quilt, Keiki faced the closed bathroom door.

That bathroom had a tricky lock that stuck when engaged; evidently, the robbers had gone inside to hide from Keiki, and now they were trapped!

The Rottweiler spun around to catch Lei's eye, then turned back to face the door, thrusting her nose against the handle, then rearing up to plant heavy paws on the door. She barked so hard that foam and spittle flew from her fangs. Lei had seldom seen anything so terrifying.

She tried to remember the signal that Josh had shown her to call Keiki to heel.

Lei snapped her fingers and pointed to the ground beside her, making sure Keiki saw the gesture. The dog backed away from the door, still facing it, still barking, but came to stand at Lei's side.

Just then, a gunshot cut across the sound of Keiki's barking and a hole appeared in the door just above the handle. Five more rapid shots followed that, and then, to Lei's horror, a hand punched through the weakened wood, reached around, then turned the handle.

Lei grabbed Keiki's collar. She couldn't let the dog charge and try to capture the man attempting to escape the bathroom, afraid she'd be shot for doing so.

She dragged Keiki back, out through Aunty's doorway, slamming the bedroom door shut. Keiki, agitated, began to bark again, trotting back and forth in front of the door as Lei threw her weight behind Aunty's fancy china hutch. She shoved the heavy piece of furniture across the bedroom door, trapping the intruder inside. Even if the robber tried to shoot his way out, he wouldn't be able to with that heavy hutch in the way.

But Aunty had a reasonably large window over the bed. Once the man realized the door was blocked, he would try to exit that way.

Maybe she and Keiki could hold him in the bedroom until the police arrived.

Lei ran to the front door, signaling for Keiki to heel; they hurried out the front door onto the porch. Sure enough, two black-clad men were clambering out of Aunty's window.

Keiki was off her leash, and the dog didn't hesitate, roaring away from Lei across the lawn. Keiki launched herself at the first of the robbers, who had reached the ground. Her aggressive assault knocked the man down; he gave a muffled cry as he hit the ground. Keiki dug her teeth into the back of his jacket, yanking and growling.

Lei was still holding the heavy poker on the porch as the second man, hanging halfway out the window by one leg, waved his pistol, trying to aim at Keiki without hitting his partner. A powerful rush of protectiveness for her dog propelled Lei forward; she ran at full speed and swung the poker as hard as she could, hitting the robber on the thigh.

The robber screamed, let go of the edge of the window, and fell the rest of the way to the ground. Lei jumped on his back and knelt there, pressing the poker, held in both hands, against the back of his neck. The pressure pushed the man's face into the grass of the yard. "Drop your weapon!" she screamed.

He let go of the gun, dropping it to the grass.

"Put your hands on the back of your head!"

The robber obeyed.

Keiki was doing a fine job on her intruder, too, standing on his back and tugging at the back of his jacket, growling as he whimpered and begged for mercy.

The headlights of two police cruisers swiveled onto their street and caught the whole scene in blinding, bright lights. Lei reached over to grab Keiki's collar. "We got them, girl."

CHAPTER TWENTY

AUNTY WAVED the *San Rafael Gazette* in front of Lei the next morning. "It sure was handy having one of the reporters at your going-away party!" She exclaimed. "Front-page news that my niece and her dog captured the robbers. What a great kickoff to your career in law enforcement!"

Lei smiled and took the paper from her aunt. She sipped from a mug of coffee, taking in the photo of herself, curls wild, holding Keiki's collar as the dog snarled in the direction of two black-clad men being led away in handcuffs. "I can't take any credit. Keiki did the whole thing herself."

"Not! That second man might have shot her if you hadn't whacked him on the leg like you did with the fire iron." Aunty glanced over at the poker, back in its holder beside the fireplace. She gave a theatrical shiver. "They say you almost broke his leg. You were very good at swinging a bat back in school."

"Would have been better to have my weapon," Lei grumbled, shaking out the paper and scanning the article. "But the stupid thing was locked in your car."

"You did fine without that gun. I'm starting a scrapbook of all of your cases. This one will go right at the beginning." Aunty opened a second copy of the paper and retrieved a pair of scissors from the kitchen drawer. "I even have a new scrapbook to get started."

"Not all of my cases," Lei said absently, still reading.

"What do you mean?" Aunty sat back down with the newspaper and scissors.

Lei bit her tongue, remembering that the events in Mexico must never be disclosed. "Never mind. I'm just sorry I couldn't make it back to the party, and you had to find out about everything when it was all over, thinking I had bailed on everyone."

"I was just worried about you. I knew it had to have been something important to keep you from our *'ohana*," Aunty said, reaching down to pat Keiki's head. "Now, you'd better hurry up so we can get you to the airport on time."

LEI PRESSED her forehead against the cool plexiglass of the airplane window. Just one of her many leis from the night before, a tuberose one, released its sweet, tropical scent as her shoulder crushed it against her neck.

Lei peered down as the jet circled, lining up with the Hilo, Hawaii runway. She took in the horseshoe shape of Hilo Bay, lined with hotels, banyan trees, and the quaint old town area. Palm trees grew larger and larger as the plane descended.

Lei's heart sped up with excitement: this was the beginning of a whole new chapter of her life, and she wanted to see everything.

The airplane touched down, bouncing lightly in a breeze off the bay, and taxiing to a stop near the small terminal. Soon Lei was making her way down the aisle, the backpack she carried instead of a purse on her back as she towed a small carry-on bag. Everything she had packed to begin her new life was in one additional suitcase she would pick up at baggage claim—she had always been a minimalist.

The plane had parked away from the terminal building, and a set of wheeled stairs was rolled up against the side of the jet.

Lei took a deep breath of the air of her birthplace as she exited, enjoying the soft, humid touch of the tropical breeze on her cheeks, even if it smelled a bit of hot asphalt and fuel. She descended the stairs, walking briskly across the tarmac to the building, then heading to baggage claim to pick up her bag. A short time later, towing her suitcase and carry-on, Lei headed for the exit—but was surprised to see an older local woman in a flowered muumuu, holding a hand-lettered cardboard sign that read 'Texeira.'

Lei approached the woman. "Are you looking for me? I'm Lei Texeira."

The woman's square tan face, framed by curly black hair scraped into a bun, broke into a smile. Lei felt a sense of familiarity.

"Lei!" The woman reached up to where a fresh plumeria garland encircled her neck. She lifted the lei off her head to drop it over Lei's curly hair. "Your aunty let me know you were arriving today, and I wanted to greet you properly. I'm your cousin Karen Texeira." She enfolded Lei in a hug that crushed both sets of flowers around Lei's neck, surrounding them in tropical fragrance. "Rosario thought it would be fun to surprise you."

"I'm so glad!" Lei smiled as she stepped back. "Great to meet you, Cuz! You must be related to Aunty Rosario and my dad."

"Yes. Your grandma was my aunty. I'm a bit older than you, but your cousin nonetheless." Karen gestured, and led Lei towards a battered green Ford truck parked at the curb. "The family'd be honored if you'd come and have dinner with us, spend the night if you like. You'll get to meet some of your relatives."

"I'm happy to. I was going to have to take a taxi to a hotel for the night. This is so much better!" Lei got into the vehicle's cab after loading her bags into the truck's bed. "Maybe you can help me find a place to rent for me and my dog. Keiki's coming over in a few months, but I'm starting my police officer training on Monday, and I need to get a place ASAP."

"Not a problem," Karen said, as she started up the truck. "Your aunty told me your situation. The family knows plenty of people in

Hilo and we've got some leads already. Consider this your hometown."

Lei smiled at her newfound cousin gratefully. "I already do."

Turn the page for a sneak peek of *Shark Cove*, Paradise Crime Mysteries Book 15.

SNEAK PEEK
SHARK COVE, PARADISE CRIME MYSTERIES BOOK 15

NOTHING interesting ever happened to Stacey Emmitt. "Seriously. Why is my life so boring?" The fifteen-year-old walked home from Maui High School, muttering to herself as the hot afternoon sun beat down on her head. She kept her eyes on her phone as she read posts from her favorite student gossip site, Wallflower Diaries. The kids written about on the site, especially homecoming king Blake Lee, seemed to have nonstop action going on in their lives.

"Ouch." Stacey tripped on a tussock of untrimmed grass, catching herself on some thorny, overgrown bougainvillea spewing out of a nearby garden—there was no sidewalk in this run-down part of Kahului. "Ow!"

"Need a ride?"

Stacey glanced up, startled, sucking on her pricked thumb.

A guy was speaking to her.

"Uh . . . I'm okay." Guys just didn't pull alongside her in fancy cars and speak to her; she didn't attract attention, hiding any looks she had under baggy jeans and oversized tees out of shyness. But yep, a guy was speaking to her: a hot guy, in a cherry red Mustang.

She shouldn't get into a car with a stranger, no matter how cute he was, or how nice the car.

"You sure? You look awfully *hot*." He drew the word out flirtatiously.

Stacey blushed. "I'm not supposed to accept rides from strangers. My parents would kill me."

"Do I look like a serial killer?" The guy had a dimple, perfect teeth, and nice muscles. He laughed. "C'mon. I'm just trying to do a good deed here." He told her his name. "What's yours?"

"Stacey," she stammered.

"See? Easy. We're not strangers anymore." The guy pulled the beautiful car into the grass ahead of her, jumped out, and opened the passenger door. "Your chariot awaits, Stacey."

She got in, hugging her heavy backpack. "Thanks."

He ran back around to his side, got in, and pulled the car onto the road. "I just went by the store and bought some cold sodas." He dug in a small cooler at her feet and pulled out a bottled Coke. "Can you open mine since I'm driving? You're welcome to one, too."

"Sure." Stacey unscrewed the bottle and handed it to him, then took one herself. She drank thirstily, draining it halfway, then hid a burp behind her hand. "You're so nice."

"That's what all the girls say." Hot Guy winked.

Five minutes later, Stacey Emmitt had passed out, her head slumped forward to rest on her backpack. The red Mustang drove out of her neighborhood, heading in another direction entirely.

Something interesting had finally happened to Stacey Emmitt, and she would never be the same.

Twenty-four hours later:

Teen girls were disappearing on Maui. The broad daylight abduction of fifteen-year-old Stacey Emmitt was the latest in a case that had been going on for months.

"I have to find whoever is doing this," Sergeant Leilani Texeira muttered aloud to her partner, Pono Kaihale, frustration tightening her jaw as she pushed through glass doors into the urban ugly rectangle of the Kahului Police Department building. "We have to get a handle on where these girls are going!"

"We're doing all we can," Pono said. "It's not all on you."

"I know." Lei blew a curl off her forehead. "I have to drop this info off to Gerry and Abe."

Usually, Lei headed straight for the elevator to the third level, where she and her partner were lucky enough to have an office on the same quiet floor as her husband, Lt. Michael Stevens—but today, she had to stop by her teammates' cubicle.

"I'll get your computer started," Pono said. Lei's aged desktop was the butt of continual jokes.

"Thanks, bro." Lei peeled off from Pono and headed onto the open 'bullpen' area, where Maui's detectives worked on everything from vice to homicide in a maze of modular units.

Gerry Bunuelos was in his unit with Abe Torufu, and Lei paused in the doorway to smile; she always enjoyed the sight of her mismatched friends together.

Bunuelos was a little over five and a half feet and a hundred and fifty pounds of wiry Filipino; he couldn't have been more different physically than massive Tongan Abe Torufu, who topped six and a half feet and two hundred fifty pounds of solid muscle. The two were engaged in animated conversation with a tall, slender, dark-haired woman wearing a detective's badge on her belt.

A visceral sense of recognition hit Lei as she gazed at the unknown detective, but when the woman turned to her, Lei couldn't place her face. "Sorry for interrupting," Lei said. "I can come back if this is a bad time."

Bunuelos stood up. "No, we were just finishing up. Lei, have you met our newest detective, Harry Clark?"

"You look familiar, but I don't believe so." Lei advanced, her hand out. "Sergeant Lei Texeira, Homicide." Clark's grip was cool and strong; her honey-brown eyes and angular face still seemed familiar. "Have we worked a case together?"

Clark winked and smiled. "As a matter of fact, we have, Lei. About sixteen years ago."

Lei stepped back, her brows snapping together. "Harriet Vierra? That Harry?"

"The very same."

Lei swallowed as her throat went dry. She had a history with this woman—a history that came back in traumatic flashes of memory now and again, the stuff of nightmares and bogeymen under the bed. Her mind buzzed with questions, none of which she could ask in front of their eager audience.

Torufu was the first to break the awkward silence. "Sixteen years ago . . . that would put you both at about legal drinking age. I wouldn't have minded meeting you girls back then."

"I'd love to hear that story!" Bunuelos chimed in.

Clark grinned. "A girl's got to keep some secrets, right, Lei?"

"Right." Lei felt wobbly, ambushed, and a little bit terrified. "We'll have to catch up sometime."

"Yep, but now is not the time or place. See you around the office!" Clark sashayed off.

Lei turned to stare after her, watching the brunette enter one of the cubicles on the other side of the room. "She's working in Vice?" Lei's voice cracked on a high note.

"Harry and her partner, Pai Opunui, just got promoted to Homicide; she came over to pick our brains about it. She transferred here from Oahu about a year ago. She's got a good reputation." One of Bunuelos's eyebrows quirked up in question. "Spill, Texeira. Did you party together back in the day?"

Best to fend off more questions with a version of the truth, rather than stoke her friends' curiosity with secretiveness.

"As a matter of fact, we did," Lei said. "One crazy, unforgettable week down in Mexico. But I haven't seen Harry since. I'm just surprised to see her again, especially as a detective—and no, I'm not telling you why." She waggled a finger at their loud groans. "On a bummer note, I came to bring you an updated file on the latest missing girl." Lei removed a folder from under her arm and handed it to Bunuelos. "I just interviewed Stacey Emmitt's parents and searched her room—they don't have a clue what might have happened to her on her way home from school. I'm not happy there's another girl gone, when we hadn't made any progress on the one before. Stacey's details are in the folder."

"I hate this case." Bunuelos's mouth tightened; he was a proud and protective father of five. "Who knows what's happening to these poor kids."

"Those 'kids' have reached the age of being totally freakin' annoying to their parents and the community in general." Torufu swiveled his chair back and forth, beefy fingertips forming a triangle that echoed the tattoos running down his ripped forearms. "Every time I haul in some brat for tagging walls, ripping off cars, or panhandling, I remember why CJ and I decided not to have kids." The thick gold wedding band on Torufu's finger was still shiny; he and their station's chief, Captain CJ Omura, had recently married.

Lei shook her head, smiling. She had two children at home and, like Bunuelos, loved her rich family life. "Thankfully, we haven't had to cross the teenage hormone bridge yet, though our son is not far from that milestone." She sobered. "I'll be in touch after you read Emmitt's file and we can set up a case review to make sure we've got everything covered and divided up."

"Got it. I'll pass this on to Abe after I read your notes." Bunuelos was already studying the folder, topped by a school photo of fifteen-year-old Stacey that the parents had provided.

Lei waved to the guys and headed for the elevator. Her gaze flicked over to Harry Clark's office in the corner of the room. Whatever had happened to the woman's adopted daughter, Malia?

The baby they'd found in Mexico during that "crazy week" they'd spent together would be about the same age of the missing victims—maybe now was a good time to warn Clark about the disappearances.

Lei changed direction and headed for Clark's cubicle. She rapped on the thin, hollow-core wooden door that gave an illusion of privacy in a network of open-ceilinged modules. "Come in!" a woman's voice called.

Lei opened the door and peered around it. Pai Opunui, a lean, shaggy-haired Hawaiian man she knew from a few cases, sat across from Clark. "Hey, Pai! Can I get a private word with Harry?"

Opunui stood up. "Perfect timing. I needed to refresh my coffee anyway." He picked up his MPD mug and left, brushing past Lei.

Lei slipped inside and shut the door, sitting on Opunui's still-warm seat. She met the brunette woman's light brown eyes. "I want to tell you about the case I'm working on."

"I thought you might want to talk about our *original* case." Harry reached for a silver-framed photo set near her computer monitor, turning it toward Lei. Inside the frame, two young girls smiled. The older one was dark-haired, brown-eyed, with tawny skin and a curvy build. The younger, almost the same height, had rippling light brown hair, hazel eyes and a freckled nose. "Malia, who you met as a baby, is on the right. The one on the left is my biological daughter, Kylie."

Lei took the frame into her hands to look at the picture more closely. "They're beautiful!"

Harry leaned back in her chair, smiling. "They're my reason to get up in the morning."

Lei glanced at Harry's left hand—no ring. "Not married? Your last name didn't used to be Clark."

Raw pain showed on Harry's face for a moment as her full mouth turned down. She shrugged, a fake-casual movement. "My husband left us about a year ago. He's a lawyer and lives in California now."

"Oh, that must be hard."

Harry nodded. "The girls have taken it badly. Particularly Kylie —she adored her dad. Malia and I . . . we're still close."

Lei set the photo frame down. "I thought I should tell you that Malia is the prime age for a ring of human traffickers that we think are operating in Hawaii. We're coordinating efforts with the FBI on all four of the major islands since every county is experiencing the disappearance of teen girls, mostly runaways. Yesterday, a girl was snatched on her way home from school."

Harry's eyes widened. "Yeah, I heard about the runaways. How is it a homicide case, though?"

"We found a body—one of the runaways who disappeared washed up in Kahului harbor with restraint marks on her wrists a few months ago. Like I said, we suspect these girls are being trafficked. I just wanted to warn you—now's a good time to keep a close eye on Malia, as well as Kylie."

Harry frowned. "Why isn't the case in the news?"

"We didn't realize this was such a big problem until recently, but with this latest disappearance, a 15-year-old on her way home from school . . . the time's come to go public. I'm bringing it up to Captain Omura in our next team meeting."

The color had drained from Harry's cheeks. "I guess human trafficking isn't just happening in Mexico." The experience they'd shared in Mexico lay between them—a dark secret Lei had done a good job of trying to forget.

Lei shook her head. "No. Unfortunately."

"Well, my girls go to a private school, Paradise Preparatory Academy, and it has pretty good security. They take a bus to and from campus. Neither of them goes anywhere alone in the community, and their father and I have drilled stranger danger into their heads as well as self-defense techniques. I'm sure they're as safe here as they would be anywhere."

Lei stood up. "I just thought I should mention it, considering Malia is close to the age of the victims."

"Thank you," Harry said. "Hey, any chance you want to come by our house after work? You can meet the baby you first saw sixteen years ago and see how she's grown up."

Lei took her phone out of her pocket and checked it. "As a matter of fact, I *can* stop by. My husband is picking our daughter up from preschool, and our son has a ride home from his soccer game with another mom. I can come by for a few minutes, sure, provided you don't live too far away."

"No. We are right up near Wailuku. Not far at all."

"Then it's a date. Give me your contact info." Harry's address and phone number were soon added to her contacts. "I'm looking forward to meeting both of your daughters."

MALIA HUNG her backpack on the hook on the wall, toed out of her shoes, and lined them up beneath it. She shrugged out of her favorite giant black hoodie, hanging it over the backpack. She still had some homework, but she'd get to it later after she checked the Wallflower texts and put some new things up on her secret gossip site.

Her sister Kylie had been dropped off earlier by a friend rather than riding the bus, and Malia spotted her backpack, thrown behind the couch. Muttering, she picked it up and hung it on the hook, then retrieved the eleven-year-old's shoes, kicked across the room, and set them next to hers. If she didn't, tomorrow morning would be awful with Kylie running around looking for missing items.

It wasn't just that her little sister was messy—it was as if she shed everything when she reached home, peeling herself like a banana and leaving the skin for Malia to slip on.

"Kylie!" Malia hollered. No answer.

She found Kylie upstairs, lying in the middle of Mom's bed, eating a bag of popcorn as the sixth grader watched a teen reality show.

"Did you hear me call you?"

"No." Kylie shoved in another handful of popcorn, chewing, her cheeks bulging like a hamster's—and she still looked way cuter than Malia would ever be.

Harry had adopted Malia in Mexico and married Peter Clark a year later. They'd thought their family complete until Kylie had come along, a total surprise. It had always given Malia a secret comfort that Kylie didn't look like Harry; their mom had Hawaiian blood that showed up in olive skin, brown hair and bold features, and Malia looked more related to her than Kylie did.

What had Malia's birth parents looked like? Who had she inherited her short stature and curvy build from? There was no one to ask; according to her mom, she'd been abandoned at an orphanage as an infant. Meanwhile, looking related to Harry saved a lot of the "I'm adopted" questions, while Kylie was the image of their good-looking dad.

"Homework before screens." Malia turned the TV off. Kylie threw a handful of popcorn at her, scowling. "Have fun picking that up." Malia turned and headed back downstairs.

Annoyed guilt, the usual feeling Kylie brought out in her, dogged her steps. It sucked to be saddled with babysitting a sister who'd been mopey and sassy ever since Dad left. No secret that Kylie was his favorite; she'd been devastated by his departure, and Malia shouldn't have to pick up the pieces he'd left behind when her own heart was bruised.

Malia had caught her parents kissing or snuggling numerous times when she was younger—but after Harry was promoted to detective and often worked twelve or more hours a day, their parents had cooled down to roommate status. Dad got more and more into his spirituality, going on "juice cleanses" and "silence retreats" and practicing meditation on the deck outside their former house on Oahu, until finally, in the kind of well-planned lawyer move Peter Clark was known for, he'd filled two suitcases and left. Just weeks later, a packet of divorce papers had arrived in the mail.

Harry had been blindsided by the whole thing. She had refused to sign the papers. They'd fought bitterly on the phone. Malia still remembered overhearing her mom imploring. "I can't raise the girls without you! Give me another chance. I'll change my job if that's what you want!"

But he hadn't believed her, and in her heart of hearts, Malia didn't either.

Harry loved her job. She ate, slept, and breathed law enforcement. Home and family were her retreat, her nest, her recharge station; she'd just taken them for granted a little too long.

"Damn you, Dad," she said aloud, taking a baggie of chicken thighs out of the freezer. Mom bought them in bulk at Costco and then separated them, just enough for each meal. Malia put the meat in the sink and glanced at the clock—4:00 p.m. Hopefully her best and only friend, Camille, would be able to talk soon.

Peter Clark used to come home from his law practice right around now, and "keep his girls company" until Mom arrived, whenever she came home.

Now it was just Malia, covering for both parents and getting popcorn thrown at her for thanks.

Kylie came schlumping down and dribbled into her chair, reluctance oozing from every pore as she opened her homework. Malia ignored this, already deep in burner phone text messages sent to the number for posting on Wallflower Diaries, her anonymous gossip blog. According to sources, Blake Lee, the homecoming king, was seeing at least three different girls. That had been three too many for the Homecoming Princess, who'd canceled their date to prom—and their confrontation made a juicy post.

Her fingers flew on her laptop's keys as Malia entered first names in conversation balloons that she pasted onto cutout yearbook photos of the girls in question and loaded into a meme maker video template. She finished the update: *"Blake L man-slut status confirmed!"*

Malia squashed the dying quiver of her own crush on Blake as she posted the graphic. Making posts into GIFs and cartoons was part of the site's appeal. To keep the material from circulating and getting her in worse trouble if she were ever tracked, Malia encrypted the posts so the address was concealed; people could see the content and leave comments, but nothing more.

Epithets began appearing right away from Blake supporters,

along with angry denials from friends of the girls. *Good.* This was a hot post. She rubbed her hands together with glee.

"What are you doing over there? Watching porn?" Kylie's eyes narrowed and her chin thrust out as she glared at Malia over her math book.

Malia snorted. "Very funny."

She shut the laptop and filled a pan and set the chicken thighs in it, adding teriyaki sauce. She took out frozen broccoli and a rice cooker, glancing at the clock. Maybe Camille would be done by now. She called her friend's cell, but it went immediately to voice mail.

An hour later, Malia turned all the food off, waiting for Mom to get home. Kylie had finished her homework and gone back upstairs by then.

She tried Camille again—no answer.

Maybe Camille's mom had taken her phone away. That had sometimes happened, like when Camille wouldn't submit to the chemical peel her mom, Regina William, had scheduled for both of them—never mind that you weren't supposed to do things to a sixteen-year-old face that you did to a fifty-year-old one.

Malia tried Camille's house phone, which rang with a sound like celestial chimes. That device was a piece of polished sculpture, a shape that didn't even look like a communication appliance. Malia could picture it there on the shiny dining room sideboard, the light of a crystal chandelier falling around it like frozen rain.

"Hello?" Regina William's breathless voice.

"Hi, Ms. William. This is Malia." Camille's mom didn't like her, so Malia was surprised when she cried, "Oh, thank God! Do you know where she is?"

"Where who is?"

"Camille! Camille's gone!" The woman's breathy voice had climbed to a screech. "She wasn't home when I got here with Pierre to do electrolysis. She's with you, right?"

"No." Malia's heart thumped with alarm. Camille was well-liked, but she was a homebody and didn't have a lot of friends she saw outside of school. Generally, she was either at her own house or Malia's. "I called this phone because she wasn't answering hers."

"But she must be with you!" Ms. William was pacing; she'd seen the elegant blonde woman do it often enough before, striding back and forth on the deep carpet of the dining room, or multitasking around the big showy house with a phone to her ear. "I can't believe this. Camille packed a bag and left a note saying she'd had it with me and the beauty treatments. She's run away!"

"What? Camille would never do that." Camille loved her mom; she might someday refuse to let her force her into a beauty queen mold, but run away? *Never.* Camille didn't like adventures. Where would she go, if not to Malia's house?

Malia felt a terrible feeling: a sock to the gut, actual nausea. What if Camille really had run away, and run away from her best friend, too?

Continue reading *Shark Cove,* Paradise Crime Mysteries Book 15: tobyneal.net/SCwb

AUTHOR NOTE

Dear Readers!

What fun to go back in time, and meet a younger, but just as bravely impulsive Lei! I enjoyed setting up some of the events that become part of her future in this prequel, and it was a special treat telling the story of how Keiki came into Lei and Aunty Rosario's life.

There are two ways you can go to read on from here! If you are new to the series, continue Lei's story in the timeline begun by this prequel, with *Blood Orchids*. Read through the stories to be ready for *Shark Cove*, #15 in the Paradise Crime Mysteries!

Or, if you're a returning fan of the series, make sure to read the excerpt of *Shark Cove*, coming soon!

As always, many thanks to my wonderful book creation team: Business manager, Jamie Davis, "Eagle Eye" Angie Lail, for copy-editing and keeping the series and characters straight, my transcriptionist Elisa, and also my fabulous Advance Review Copy (ARC) team, who help us find typos! You all rock and keep me coming back to the page.

Until next time, I'll be writing!

Much aloha,

TOBY NEAL

FREE BOOKS

Join my mystery and romance lists and receive free, full-length, award-winning novels *Torch Ginger & Somewhere on St. Thomas.*

tobyneal.net/TNNews

TOBY'S BOOKSHELF

PARADISE CRIME SERIES

Paradise Crime Mysteries
Blood Orchids

Torch Ginger

Black Jasmine

Broken Ferns

Twisted Vine

Shattered Palms

Dark Lava

Fire Beach

Rip Tides

Bone Hook

Red Rain

Bitter Feast

Razor Rocks

Wrong Turn

Shark Cove

Paradise Crime Mysteries Novella

Clipped Wings

Paradise Crime Mystery
Special Agent Marcella Scott
Stolen in Paradise

Paradise Crime Suspense Mysteries
Unsound

Paradise Crime Thrillers
Wired In
Wired Rogue
Wired Hard
Wired Dark
Wired Dawn
Wired Justice
Wired Secret
Wired Fear
Wired Courage
Wired Truth
Wired Ghost
Wired Strong
Wired Revenge
Coming 2021

ROMANCES
Toby Jane

The Somewhere Series
Somewhere on St. Thomas
Somewhere in the City
Somewhere in California

The Somewhere Series

Secret Billionaire Romance
Somewhere in Wine Country
Somewhere in Montana
Date TBA
Somewhere in San Francisco
Date TBA

A Second Chance Hawaii Romance
Somewhere on Maui

YOUNG ADULT

Standalone
Island Fire

NONFICTION
TW Neal

Memoir
Freckled
Open Road

ABOUT THE AUTHOR

Kirkus Reviews calls Neal's writing, *"persistently riveting. Masterly."*

Award-winning, USA Today bestselling social worker turned author Toby Neal grew up on the island of Kaua`i in Hawaii. Neal is a mental health therapist, a career that has informed the depth and complexity of the characters in her stories. Neal's mysteries and thrillers explore the crimes and issues of Hawaii from the bottom of the ocean to the top of volcanoes. Fans call her stories, *"Immersive, addicting, and the next best thing to being there."*

Neal also pens romance and romantic thrillers as Toby Jane and writes memoir/nonfiction under TW Neal.

Visit tobyneal.net for more ways to stay in touch!
or
Join my Facebook readers group, *Friends Who Like Toby Neal Books,* for special giveaways and perks.

Made in the USA
Middletown, DE
20 December 2022